IT
BREAKS
MARBLE

Chapter 1

Double Espresso, Please

The date is Wednesday, June 7th, 2023. Giuseppe 'Joe' DiGrasso, a tall slender man with slicked black hair and a nose the size of Rhode Island, slides into his cherry red '62 Alfa Romeo and pulls out of his driveway. He lives in a chic Villa on the coast of Sicily, Palermo with his wife and two daughters, all of whom are sound asleep as he drives off into the Sicilian sunrise.

Tony better be ready to go when I get there, he thinks. *If he did something stupid and got more time, Vinny is gonna be so pissed. Hell,* I'm *gonna be so pissed.* Joe shakes his head to clear his thoughts, turns up the music, and keeps driving.

Finally, Joe arrives at a prison. Tony, a tall, muscular man with short black hair, and a nose not quite as large as Joe's, is already outside with his belongings.

"Wow, I don't think I've ever seen you up and ready this early in the morning, Tone!" Joe exclaims. They embrace in a familiar hug. "How were the past six months, my brother?" Joe asks.

"Fine, Joe. Would have been a helluva lot betta if you got me those cigarettes like I asked you," said Tony, as he poked Joe in the chest.

The two brothers walk towards Joe's '62 Romeo. "Now, Tone," said Joe, "you know there is no possible way to get cigarettes into that prison without being sloppy and gettin' caught. You know I don't do sloppy work. Sloppy work is how you wound up in this prison in the first place."

As they slide into the car, Tony says, “Yeah, yeah. I know you’re a perfectionist, Joe. But sometimes you just gotta take a chance and do something special for your family. Especially for your older brother.”

Joe starts the car, turns to Tony, and pointedly says, “I do something special for my family every day. It’s called staying out of prison. Taking chances is *not* something I do, nor is it something Vinny and Sal would ever approve of. You know how hard I have to work to become the boss as the *younger* brother? Plus, you think once I *am* the boss, I can take chances, make mistakes, risk going to PRISON? No. No way. I’ve worked too hard to take a chance like that. If this family is going to stay intact, one of us needs to be the smart one. The *responsible* one.”

Tony smiles at Joe. “I’ve missed your uptight ass, Joe.”

Joe smiles back at Tony. “I’ve missed your irresponsible ass, Tony. Now let's go get some coffee. Sal is waiting for us. He wants to update you on what you’ve missed while on the inside. Apparently, Sal and Vin have a hot new project for us to work on."

Tony sighs, "Agh. Sal Conti is one uptight ass I did not miss."

Joe smirks and drives off.

1

Sitting in the coffee bar in a booth is a short and slender man, with thin, gray hair and narrow wire glasses on his face. Even at the relatively young age of 45 years old, he could not stop father time from aging his hair. He is sipping an espresso and reading an American newspaper. The man is Salvatore 'Sal' Conti, the Underboss of the DiGrasso family. While Sal does not share the DiGrasso last name with the rest of the higher-ups in the family, he is number two in charge behind the Don, Vincenzo 'Vinny' or 'Vin' DiGrasso. Of course, he is still family – albeit extended. As Vinny's nephew, Sal had an in but needed to prove his loyalty. Especially considering he would be competing with Vinny's two sons, Giuseppe and Anthony, for positions within the family. Sal was especially worried about his future when Vinny and his first wife, Sylvia divorced. Sal Conti is the son of Sylvia's sister; therefore, when Sylvia left, Sal had concerns that he too, would be out of the picture; however, this was not the case. Vinny is a very loyal man to those who exhibit loyalty to him first. Sal proved himself as the most loyal to Vinny in his early days as the Don. Especially while Vinny's sons were too young to be involved in the business. Although Sal was arguably too young to be in the business at the time he joined – he was only seventeen years old. Of course, Anthony was twelve, and Joe was nine, so having them join was out of the question entirely.

A bell at the front door of the coffee shop dings. Sal Conti takes his glasses off and brings his gaze from the newspaper, up toward the door. He sees Joe and Tony walk in and smiles at them. The men smile back and slide into the booth.

A waitress comes over to them, smiles, and asks, "Can I get you boys anything?"

Sal slams the remainder of his espresso and says, "Yeah darlin'. Three double espressos, please."

The waitress nods. “You got it, Sal,” she says and walks toward the bar.

Tony looks at Sal with a raised eyebrow. “Careful there, Sal. All that coffee is gonna make your asshole explode like Mount Etna.”

Sal and Joe both chuckle and shake their heads. “Still as immature as you were before they locked you up, eh Tone?” said Sal.

Tony chuckles and shrugs. “Yeah, I guess,” he says.

Joe raises an eyebrow and asks, “The fuck you reading there, Sal? Is that an American newspaper?”

Tony looks down at what Sal is holding. “Why you readin’ a paper, Sal? Everything is digital nowadays. You gotta change with the times, old man.”

Sal points to his glasses. “See these?” he asks. “These would be twice as thick if I was staring at a screen all day. The paper is fine.” Sal holds up the newspaper. “This is what I’m reading.” On the front page is an article titled “Could a Coffee Farm Cartel Save the Coffee Industry?”

“Hah, El Chapo writing articles now or somethin’? Why you reading this, Sal?” asked Tony.

“It piqued your father’s interest. You would know that if you weren’t on the inside,” said Sal.

Tony’s face darkens.

“Plus, what is of interest to your father, is of interest to me. Ergo, that is why I am reading this article,” said Sal.

Joe asks, “Why is Pops interested in what the cartel is doing? Are they interferin’ with business? I didn’t think we had any dealings with the coffee industry.”

“No, it’s not referring to a cartel in the way you two are thinkin’ about. And no, we don't have any dealings in the coffee industry,” said Sal. “Your father believes there has been a long-overlooked opportunity.”

“In coffee?” asks Tony.

“Indeed,” says Sal. He turns the newspaper over to the two men sitting side by side in the booth across from him. He says, “I know you two are well-versed in Cosa Nostra history.”

Joe and Tony both nod their heads, looking both intrigued and confused.

He continues, “Think back to the ’70s and ’80s. We owned the lions fuckin’ share of the heroin distribution. Especially in the United States. I mean, we basically owned New York, Miami, Chicago, you name it.”

The waitress walks over again. “Here you are, gentleman. Three double espressos.” She hands a tiny cup to all three men at the table.

“Thanks, darlin’,” said Sal.

Joe and Tony both smile and nod at the waitress.

“My pleasure,” she says and then walks away.

Tony scoffs. “Jesus Christ. Took long enough, eh?” he says.

Sal looks at Tony and pointedly says, “It takes time to do good work. Patience is a virtue. Maybe a virtue you could practice. Especially now that you've seen where rushed, sloppy work can take you."

There is a moment of silence at the table. Tony's fists clench, turning his knuckles white. His face turns to stone. Joe can see Tony's anger bubbling and intervenes. He says, "Sal, what interest does Vin have in coffee?"

Sal replies, "As I was saying. We owned the vast majority of the heroin distribution. Times were good. Of course, other gangs dabbled in the drug distribution. The Colombians owned coke, the Mexicans owned grass, but heroin… that belonged to us. To Cosa Nostra. Now, let me ask you boys a question. Why did our ownership of the heroin distribution fizzle out relative to the '70s and '80s?"

Joe responds, "American fuckin' law enforcement. That's why."

"Precisely," says Sal. "American fuckin' law enforcement. Heroin is too high profile. It grabs the attention of too many people. I mean, the Americans have an entire governmental agency watchdoggin' that shit for Christ's sake." Sal shoots back his espresso and continues. "You see, our ancestors worked hard, but not smart."

Tony chimes in. "Watch it, Sal. That's *our* ancestors you're talkin' about," he says pointing to himself and Joe.

"There is no 'we' in the ancestry I'm talkin' about." Sal replies, "I distinctly remember the Don before your father. He had a nephew faithfully serve as his underboss too. Just like me. This *is* our ancestry, Tony. Now, may I continue? This is important to your father."

Tony sits back and crosses his arms.

Sal continues. "Our ancestors worked hard, but not smart. They didn't think about what happens when they scale their operation. Heroin would have been fine if we kept our network to Sicily. Hell, it probably would have been fine if we kept it just to Europe. But worldwide? No, no, no. That's what they got wrong. When the business you're doing is wildly illegal all over the world, you got too many eyes on you. The proper way to scale an operation is to go into something low-key – something mundane.

Then, we can do what we do. We can protect our business interests, without having to worry about some DEA agent hovering over our shoulder."

Joe intervenes. "Yeah but, Sal. Drugs are addictive. Once people get their hands on it, they need it. Products that are 'low-key' won't ensure people keep coming back for more at all costs. I mean we were jacking up prices every three months with heroin and had no loss in sales. How can you guarantee that kind of security with something *legal*?"

"Look around you," says Sal. "There is one crop on the earth that people are *addicted* to, that is *legal* in every country, and that *everybody* consumes. Coffee."

Tony gives Joe a glance that says 'Are you fucking kidding me?' "Coffee?" says Tony.

"Coffee," says Sal. He points to the newspaper and says, "Take a look at this article." To the right of the title, is a group of people protesting outside of a Starbucks. Sal continues. "It talks about how coffee farmers are experiencing growing price pressure from increased competition with other farmers. See, coffee mostly comes from emerging market countries. In these countries, there is a growing amount, but not a ton of opportunities for work. However, agriculture is a low barrier to entry for people to make a buck or two in emerging markets. What are some of the top crop exports? Sugar, cocoa, and *coffee*. Now, because growing these crops is a relatively low barrier to entry, everyone is trying to do it. With more competition, comes greater price pressure. Supply is essentially outpacing demand. It's a buyer's market. Importers are buying premium coffee for one US dollar a pound, and selling it for six dollars a *cup* in America. The article talks about farmers wanting an organization to control the supply being exported. A cartel, if you will." Sal pauses. "You boys familiar with OPEC?"

Joe nods and Tony shakes his head. "Well," says Sal. "OPEC is an oligopoly, or cartel, of countries that control the majority of the world's oil supply. In order to keep prices at what they deem a sustainable level, they control the *amount* supply being exported around the world. Less supply means higher prices. These coffee farmers want an OPEC for coffee."

Joe holds his hand up to stop Sal. He says, "Wait, wait, wait. Sal, are you saying you want us to create an organization to control the coffee supply? What is in it for the family?"

"Well," said Sal. "We need to buy a few coffee farms. Make a few investments. Specifically in countries that have high exports relative to the rest of the world. And the cheaper the better obviously, so ideally in a place where our money can go a long way. Once we buy the coffee farms for cheap, we organize. We'll start in one country. Buy the largest farms, and let the next largest farmers there know what we intend on doing – get them on our side. We'll explain that setting regulations on supply will increase their profits. Not only that, but supply limitations will reduce the number of competition. The small guys can't compete with the large farms if supply is limited because they can't produce the crop for as cheap as the big guys. It's a win-win. Well, for the big farms anyway. Once we get the farmers on our side, we begin. We lobby, or campaign for politicians to set regulations for how much coffee is exported, when it's exported, how much it's sold for, and so on."

Tony intervenes. "Sal, if it is as easy as you're making it sound, why hasn't anyone else done this yet?"

"Glad you asked," said Sal. "Because no coffee farmer or organization has the resources, power, or influence we have."

There is another moment of silence at the table. Tony is staring at his cold espresso, trying to make sense of it all. Joe shoots the last bit of his espresso, and asks, "Vin likes this idea?"

Sal replies, "Likes it? It was *his* idea. He loves the idea. In fact, he wants us all to meet at his house later this week to discuss implementation. My boys, Gio and Nick are gonna be there too. Sounds like he wants you four to spearhead the operation."

Tony says, “You’re really getting your sons involved with the family? How old are they, twelve?”

“Eighteen and twenty,” said Sal. “Older than I was when I joined. Don’t worry, Tone. They will be your soldiers. Your direct reports.”

Joe says, “Well, it sounds like the biggest project any of us have taken on during our service to the family. We’ll take all the help we can get. What time this week did he want everyone to meet?”

“He wants us all to have dinner at his place Friday,” said Sal.

Joe nods and stands up from the booth. “Speakin’ of which. Come on, Tone. We should go visit Pops now that you’re out. I told him we’d stop by sometime today.”

Tony slides out of the booth. “You boys give your father my best, eh?” said Sal.

“You know we will, old man,” said Joe.

Sal smirks. “I’m only eight years older than you! Old man my ass.”

Joe grins, puts one hundred Euros on the table for the espressos, and heads for the door with Tony.

2

Once the men are outside the coffee bar Tony asks, "What was that about?"

"What?" Joe asks. "The one hundred Euros you put on the table! What, did the price of espresso skyrocket while I was on the inside? If so, then I think this whole coffee cartel thing actually might be a very good idea," Tony said, sarcastically.

They reach the '62 Romeo and get inside. Joe says, "It's a statement. Sometimes, Sal needs a reminder that although he is ahead of us on the hierarchy, he doesn't have the familial connection we do. He doesn't have the access to capital we do." Joe turns to face Tony. "He doesn't have our blood."

Tony smiles and responds "You're a *quiet* menace, Joe. Let your actions do the talkin' eh?"

"Yeah, somethin' like that," Joe replied.

With that, the men drive off to visit their father.

3

Thirty-five minutes later, Joe and Tony are standing on the front porch of a large, beautiful Villa on the beach. Their father, Vincenzo "Vinny" or "Vin" DiGrasso lives in the aforementioned Villa on the outskirts of Palermo, overlooking the Tyrrhenian Sea. Joe knocks on the white marble door. The gold doorknob turns, and standing in the doorway is a young thirty-year-old, beautiful, dark-haired, olive-skinned Sicilian woman.

"Hey boys!" exclaimed the woman.

"Hey Jules," they each replied. She steps aside to let them inside.

Julia DiGrasso is a model from the small town of Salemi, Sicily. She moved to Milan to pursue her dreams of becoming a model, where she met Vinny DiGrasso. Vinny was on a trip with his wife at the time, Sylvia. Vinny and Sylvia got married young, but over the years, their marriage grew stale. Sylvia began to resent the family business and began to regret how they earned their riches. Vinny could sense this and grew spiteful. He would think, *I work my ass off to provide a wonderful life for my family, but nobody appreciates it.* He would spoil Sylvia with jewelry, which she loved in their twenties and thirties. Although as time passed, she began to resent the jewelry too. All she could think of was the blood that must have been spilled for those gifts.

During the trip to Milan, Vinny, and Sylvia got into a fight at dinner. Sylvia left the date and called a taxi to go back to their hotel, alone. That is when Vinny looked up from his plate, and noticed a young, attractive woman staring at him from across the restaurant. At the time, Julia was twenty, and Vinny was fifty-two.

Slowly but surely, Syvlia started questioning why Vinny was out so late. Usually, during busy work weeks, he would be back before the sun crested over the horizon. However, in the five years following that fateful night in Milan, Vinny had many late nights at work that kept him from coming home until nine o'clock in the morning.

Even with her doubts, Sylvia stayed with Vinny. It wasn't until Vinny got so sloppy with the affair that Syvlia found a pair of Julia's panties in his pockets while doing his laundry. That is when she finally left him.

Now, ten years after the night in Milan, Vinny and Julia are married and living together.

"He's out back, having a cigar," Julia said.

The boys follow her through the house to the back patio. In the living room, Joe and Tony look through the floor-to-ceiling windows that overlook the back patio and see their father sitting in a lounge chair by a kidney-shaped pool. Vinny is smoking a cigar with one hand, and holding a brandy in his other. He's wearing Versace aviators, swim trunks, and a floral button-down short-sleeve that is unbuttoned.

Vinny likes to flaunt his body sometimes. As a sixty-two-year-old, he's kept in great shape. Many of his peers and colleagues have developed bellies over the years from the heinous amounts of food they eat. Vinny likes food too – he is Sicilian after all –

but he knows his limit. He also makes it a point to work out frequently, exhibited by his tall athletic build. Maybe that is why Julia fell in love with him. Vinny is seemingly the only wealthy man in Sicily that hasn't gorged himself into a tomato. That, and the fact that he is also seemingly the only one with a full head of hair. Julia adores his full, albeit thinning, set of salt and pepper-colored hair.

The boys walk out to the back patio. Tony is a little taken aback. He almost forgot how beautiful the Villa is. The backyard not only has the pool, but a hot tub surrounded by palm trees, and a view that overlooks the bright blue Tyrrhenian Sea.

Vinny looks up from his brandy, rips his sunglasses off, and exclaims, "Joe! Tony! My boys!" He runs over to them, arms wide with his cigar and brandy still in each hand. He hugs Tony first. "I've missed you, my son," said Vinny.

"Thanks, Pops. I missed you too. And ole' big-nose over here," Tony said and pointed his thumb toward Joe. Joe and Vinny exchange an embrace while chuckling at what Tony just said.

"He didn't get that nose from me. I don't know *where* he got it. Hah! Come, boys. Come sit down," Vinny said while he made a gesture toward the other pool chairs.

Each one takes a lounge chair, and they sit in a semi-circle around the bend of the kidney-shaped pool. They all put their feet up, and get horizontal in the chairs.

Julia walks out in a white sundress, holding a cigar and a brandy in each hand. She hands Joe and Tony one from each hand.

Joe smiles. "Thanks, Julia," he said.

"Yeah, thanks Jules," remarks Tony.

"Anytime boys," she said as she sauntered off toward the beach from their patio.

Joe pulls out a lighter, lights his and Tony's cigar, and takes a big puff.

Tony asks, "You're still livin' it up here huh, Pops?"

Vinny replies, "Yes, Anthony. Still livin' it up. Happy to be out?"

"Yeah, definitely. Especially when it means I get to be in this paradise," said Tony.

Vinny smirks. "Well, hopefully, that means you learned your lesson, eh?"

Tony replies, "Yeah, yeah. No more sloppy work. I'm a new man."

"Good," said Vinny. There is a moment of silence as the three men embrace the hot Sicilian, summer sun.

Joe looks at Vinny and asks, "You heard from Nicolette recently?"

Vinny sighs. "No," he said. "You know your sister hasn't spoken to me more than five times since your mother and I separated. Why do you think that would have changed all of a sudden?"

Joe and Tony exchange a look. "She's gettin' married, Dad," said Joe.

Then, silence. Not a word from anyone. The three men continue basking in the Sicilian sun on the back patio of Vincenzo DiGrasso's beautiful Villa. Vinny puts his sunglasses back on and takes a sip of his brandy. He swallows the warm, dark, liquor, and a tear falls from his eye. The tear streams down his face and past the rim of his sunglasses, as he reminisces about the day his baby girl, Nicolette was born.

Chapter 2

We're Going to Vietnam

Many hours later, Joe finds himself back at home. He walks in through the garage and is greeted by his wife, Josephine. Josephine DiGrasso stands at about 5'10, showcasing an athletic build. Hailing from Como on mainland Italy, Josephine flaunts fair skin, blonde hair, and blue eyes. Traits the Sicilian locals do not see frequently. She may as well have been Swiss for all they could tell.

Ever since Joe started making serious money with the family, she felt safe to quit her job and focus on her dreams of becoming a professional tennis player. She's not half bad either. As one of the top 5 women in Sicily, she has been getting a lot of recognition. She was invited to a few tournaments in Rome and Milan to compete against some of the top women throughout the rest of Italy; however, competing in those big cities is a different story. She still has yet to make a name for herself in that arena.

When Joe walks into the kitchen from the garage, he sees Josephine putting the finishing touches on dinner. Sicilian chicken spiedini and a giant bowl of salad. She is leaning over the white marble countertop sprinkling parmesan over the salad.

When she hears footsteps she looks up and smiles. “Hi sweetie,” she said.

“Hey babe,” said Joe.

“How is your brother?” she asks. “Happy to be home?”

Joe nods. “Yeah, he seems happy. I think he forgot how beautiful my father's house is. He was like a kid in a candy store.”

Josephine smirks and asks, “Are you sure it wasn’t Julia he was gawking at? Even Tony is too old for her.”

Joe laughs.

“You were gone for quite some time,” said Josephine. “Everything okay?”

Joe replies, “Yeah everything is okay. Just discussing some new business developments.”

“Ah, good,” said Josephine with a smile. “Momma needs a new racket, some new shoes, some new clothes.” Josephine walks over to Joe and puts her arms around his neck.

Joe puts his arms around her waist and says, “Didn’t we just get you like ten new tennis outfits?”

Josephine replies, “Eleven. And I haven’t gotten a new racket in a while.”

There is a thunder of footsteps, and two little girls appear from the staircase, sprinting toward Joe with their arms wide. “Daddyyyyy!” they yell in unison.

Joe responds, “Sara! Anna! How are my beautiful girls?”

The three of them embrace one another. Sara, the eldest of the two, replies “Good! Mommy took us to her tennis practice and she kicked butt!”

Joe says, “I’m not surprised! Your mother kicks my butt every time we play too.”

“Alright girls, why don't you take your seats at the table so we can eat,” said Josephine.

“Smells terrific,” said Joe and then leans into his wife for a kiss. Joe takes his seat at the table with Josephine, and they all enjoy a lovely, family dinner.

1

At the same time Joe is walking into his kitchen from the garage, Tony is walking into his bachelor pad of a studio in the heart of Palermo. He is on the top floor of a six-story building, in a corner unit. There are floor-to-ceiling windows that wrap around the corner to give a fabulous view of the city lights. In the living room is a couch that could fit twelve people, and a large marble coffee table with gold legs. The apartment is well-furnished and has the potential to be a very classy place. The only issue is that it is a pigsty. There are dirty clothes on the floor, and couch. Dirty dishes fill the sink and cover the kitchen table, creating a rancid smell that has been culminating ever since he got locked away six months prior.

Tony sighs and shakes his head. *Man, it smells like Sal's ballsack in here*, he thinks. As he enters the apartment, something catches his eye. He walks into the living room and picks up one of the many plates from the coffee table to examine it. There is a clump of old mozzarella growing black mold on the plate. Tony retches and thinks, *No, this can't be me anymore. I gotta get it together. No more sloppy work. No more sloppy living. It starts now.*

Before he knows it, Tony is cleaning the apartment. Two hours go by. Three. Four hours. He is on a roll. Cleaning every crevice possible. Making the place spotless. The windows are so clear, he would have thought there was no glass there if he didn't know any better. Five hours into cleaning, the place is unrecognizable. Tony almost forgot the top of his coffee table is a beautiful white, speckled marble instead of a dusty gray.

He plops down on the couch, exhausted from his maniacal cleaning episode. He then grabs the remote and turns on his oversized TV. As the lights flash from the screen, Tony's eyes begin to flutter. Ten minutes later, he is sound asleep. He forgot how easy it is to fall asleep in the comfort of your own home.

Two days pass, and Tony hasn't gotten up from the couch at all except to eat and shit. He can't get over how comfortable he has been the past forty-eight hours. His couch which cost him ten thousand Euros is a hell of a lot nicer than his prison cot. *Keepin' a clean house is pretty easy I guess*, he thinks. *All you gotta do is sit around. You can't make a mess when you just sittin' around.*

Tony was laying down, watching *Scarface* for the third time when he heard his phone ring. *Shit. It's Joe*, he thinks. He deliberates on accepting or declining the call. He's just so comfortable. He doesn't need uptight Joe stressing him out right now. His thumb hovers over the answer button then hits decline. Two seconds later his phone rings. It's Joe again. Tony sighs and hits the answer button.

He answers, "Hey Joe–"

"What the fuck, Tony? You ignorin' my calls? What's the matter with you? Joe shot back.

"I'm not ignoring you, Joe. I just didn't feel like gettin' chewed out is all," said Tony.

Joe replies, "Well if I didn't chew you out, you woulda missed dinner with Pops, eh?"

Tony shoots upright and looks outside. The sun is setting. He then looks at his watch. It is 6:30 pm. "Shit, is it Friday already?!" he asks frantically.

Joe answers, "You don't even know what fuckin' day it is, Tony? My ten and seven-year-old daughters know what fuckin' day it is. Get dressed. We gotta leave now. I'm outside your apartment in the Romeo. Get your ass out here."

"Alright alright," said Tony as he hung up the phone.

He runs into the bedroom closet and quickly grabs a clean button-down short-sleeve shirt. Instead of taking the time to unbutton the shirt, put it on, and rebutton it, he simply slides it over his head, fully buttoned. *Oof*, he thought as he slipped into the shirt. *Is that me?* he wondered. Tony lifts his right arm, takes a big whiff of his underarm, and almost passes out. He runs into the bathroom and quickly applies deodorant. As he was running out of his apartment, something occurred to him. *Shit!* he thought. Tony runs back into his apartment, grabs his cell phone sitting on the marble coffee table that is finally white after all these years, and darts back out.

Joe is sitting in his red 1962 Alfa Romeo, waiting for Tony. Finally, he appears. Tony opens the passenger seat door and slides into the car. "Hey Joe," said Tony, out of breath.

Joe looks at Tony, annoyed. "Hey, Tone. Busy day?" he asked.

"Oh you know, just some cleaning. Forgot how nice it is to be home so I was enjoying the whole 'not having a roommate in a cell' thing," he replied.

Joe shifts the car into drive and peels out of his parking spot on the curb.

2

The boys pull up to Vinny's villa at seven o'clock. Tony glances at Joe and remarks "Looks like we are right on time, eh?" and lets out a chuckle.

Joe shakes his head, annoyed. The brothers exit the car and walk up to the white marble door at the entrance of the house. Tony raps on the door.

A few seconds later, Julia answers the door.

"Hey boys!" she exclaimed with a big smile.

"Hey, Jules. Are you eating with us tonight?" asked Joe.

She says, "Unfortunately, I will not be joining you boys. I heard it was a business meeting so I quickly called some girlfriends to come to eat dinner on the back patio and enjoy a night in the hot tub after. I just get so bored at those 'business meetings'." Julia laughs and adds, "Plus, I feel useless. I never have anything to add!" Julia waves them into the house. "Come on in boys!"

Joe and Tony enter the house and immediately hear voices neither of them recognizes.

They walk into the foyer, on their way to the kitchen. Julia departs from them and continues toward the door to the back patio. The voices get louder.

One of the unfamiliar voices belts, "I mean Gio, come on, you tryin' to be fuckin' Capone or somethin'? Why you wearin' that eye sore?"

The brothers hear laughter, both of which they recognize. One is their father, Vinny, and the other is Sal.

Joe and Tony enter the kitchen and four pairs of eyes fix on them. Vinny, Sal, and Sal's two sons Nicholas and Giovanni Conti. They are all munching on Arancini and drinking Chianti. One of the two boys Joe and Tony do not recognize, has red sauce on his chin and a fedora on his head. This is Giovanni Conti. Gio is a tall, slim, young man. You could say he doesn't quite have the street smarts of most eighteen-year-olds, but he has twice the heart, and the eagerness to learn. The other, Nicholas, is still grinning ear to ear from his joke. He has a tall, athletic build with dark curly hair that his girlfriend Sofia, just adores. He has done some small side projects with Sal over the last year or so and has proven to be a quick, clean, and efficient worker. Sal has told Vinny about the great work his son is capable of. Now, Vinny is eager to see it for himself.

Vinny waves his arms in a 'get over here' motion. "Boys! Have a seat!" he exclaimed, smiling.

Joe and Tony take a seat next to each other at the beautiful, long, hardwood kitchen table with the rest of the guys. A woman walks over and puts a plate of warm olives and cold prosciutto on the table.

As she walks back to the stove, Vinny says, "Thanks Maria. The arancini were exquisite," and then puts his thumb and three fingers to his lips and kisses them as he opens his hand.

Maria turns back, smiles, and continues to work on the food at the stove.

Sal looks in the direction of Joe and Tony and says, "Joe, Tony. These are my two sons, Nick and Gio," and points to the unfamiliar faces. "They are the ones I mentioned would be helping us with our new business venture."

Joe and Tony exchange pleasantries with the young men. Sal continues, "Nick helped me with a few low-key projects this past year and has done a great job. This will be Gio's first time with this kind of work, but I think you'll find him to be a quick learner."

Joe and Tony look at Gio's young face. Tony has to hold back laughter every time he looks at Gio and his fedora. The hat and young face remind him of a goofy kid he went to grade school with. Great kid, but naive as all hell.

Maria walks back to the kitchen table and sets down a heaping bowl of tortellini with cream sauce, and an equally heaping plate of chicken parmesan. "Thank you, Maria. Thank you!" said Vinny. "Now if you don't mind, we're gonna get to business."

Maria responds, "Of course. Have a great night, gentlemen!" and walks to the front door to go home for the night.

"I'll tell ya," said Vinny. "It's been great having Maria around this past year. Since Julia hates to cook, having Maria do it has been good for both of us."

Sal replies, "Yeah, and look at this! A beautiful feast we have here."

Gio is staring past Sal and Vinny, both of whom are sitting across from him, gazing out the window to the back patio. He says "Yeah. Beautiful."

Sal and Vinny both raise an eyebrow and turn around in unison. They see Julia and four of her tall Model friends in small bikinis getting into the hot tub. Nick sees what is going on, turns to Gio, and says, "You need a girlfriend, my guy."

"Nah," said Gio, still gazing out the window. "I'm focused on work. Making a name for myself. Girls are just a distraction."

Nick replies, "Sounds like something someone who has a hard time pulling girls would say."

Tony laughs at this. Gio breaks his gaze and punches Nick in the arm.

Sal cuts in and says, "Alright, alright. Calm down, boys. Let's get to business." All five pairs of eyes fixated on Sal and the men lean in, ready to hear the plan that will forever be ingrained in Cosa Nostra's history. "I've given everyone here the quick and dirty idea of this new venture. Me and Vin spent many nights coming up with a detailed plan, so pay attention. This won't be a simplistic operation."

Tony cuts in, "It's coffee, Sal. I mean, come on. We've worked in way more complex industries."

Sal shoots back. "No, you have not. This plan will require politics, partnerships, and an understanding of fuckin' economics. We aren't doing this the way we did heroin. We're gonna be smart about this. Play for the long haul."

Tony crosses his arms and sits back.

Sal continues. "As I was saying, this won't be a simple operation. We start by determining the coffee-producing country in which we want to start. Ideally, a country that has high coffee exports relative to the rest of the world. Now, I have a question for the table. Who here knows the top two coffee-producing countries in the world?"

Nick says, "I'm always seeing Colombian roast at the coffee shops nowadays, so that's got to be one of the two, right?"

"Wrong," said Sal. "Good guess though. No, number one is Brazil, and number two is Vietnam."

Tony lets out a short laugh. "Hah! Vietnam? Sal, what the fuck you talkin' about?"

"It's true, Son," said Vinny. "Second largest coffee producer in the world behind Brazil."

Tony looks flabbergasted. He crosses his arms again and lets Sal continue.

Sal says, "We looked at potentially buying a farm in Brazil – it being the largest producer and all – but a lot of Westerners have been buying up coffee farms there. The market is too hot. Farms are expensive. So we went down the list. Vietnam coffee farms are unknown outside of the coffee community. Nobody is buying farms there for 'eco-tourism'. They are still cheap as shit – especially with the exchange rate between the Euro and the Dong."

Gio and Tony start laughing.

Joe looks at the two of them. "Really, Tone? You're forty years old and you're still laughing at that shit?"

Tony shrugs, and Gio's face turns as deep of red as the Chianti they are drinking, and they quiet down.

Sal goes on. "We then go searching for a few coffee farms we want to buy or make a sizable investment in – an investment large enough that we retain control of the operations. We have to be deliberate in the farms we buy or invest in. It is important we get the biggest, most influential farms in Vietnam, that way we catch the attention of the ICO members. We need to have power and influence over them."

Joe asks, "ICO?"

"Ah, yes," said Sal. "The ICO is the International Coffee Organization. They are the governing body of the coffee industry, worldwide. They set the rules, regulations, and strategies of the coffee industry for the countries involved. The ICO has many committees, but the one we are focused on is the International Coffee Council. This council is the highest authority in the organization, and the most influential. The council is composed of representatives from each member country. The representatives are all politicians because they have to be government officials to enact the agreed-upon laws in their respective countries. We need the Vietnamese representatives to do our bidding. We have them convince the members of the council to set supply restrictions to benefit their country's farmers. Limited supply means higher prices the crop can be sold. The governing officials will be heroes to the big farmers."

"What about the small farmers?" asked Nick. The group turns their attention to him. "What if the officials of lower coffee-producing countries block that proposal? Doesn't regulation on supply make it tougher to enter the market for the little guys? Economies of scale or some shit."

Sal smiles and says, "The brain on this fuckin' kid, eh?! Great question. The council passes proposals via general consensus. If it doesn't pass the first time around, we'll have to do a little convincing for enough people to gain a consensus."

Gio asks, "How can we convince them to join our side though?"

Sal replies, "Cosa Nostra has our ways, Gio. You'll figure that out in time." He continues, "Once we have our supply restrictions in place, we will lower our prices until the little farmers can't match it without taking a loss, and watch them go out of business, and then reverse our supply restrictions so that we have the market share and the price control. If more countries try to enter the market, we will implement the restrictions again. It'll likely just be us and Brazil."

The room grows silent to digest the information. Then, the back patio door opens and there is suddenly chatter and laughter filling the house. Julia and her friends walk into the kitchen wearing short, cover-up pool dresses. Julia makes a straight face and says, “So serious,” mocking the guys. The guy's attention turns to Julia and the ladies. “We’re going downstairs, just wanted to say hi,” she said and then smiled at Vinny.

Vinny smiles back and says, “Sounds good, baby. Have fun.” The women walk out of the kitchen and down the stairs.

In the kitchen amongst the men, there is another moment of silence. Sal breaks the silence. “Alright guys hit me with the questions, what are you all thinking about?”

Tony speaks first. How do we even begin looking for farms to buy? We don’t know a thing about the coffee industry, and we know even less about Vietnam. How do we know a good farm from a bad farm? How do we get in contact with the owners?”

Vinny replies to his son. “Tone, did you forget something while you were on the inside? This family has *connections*. Show them, Sal”.

Sal reaches into the breast pocket of his shirt and pulls out a folder piece of paper. Sal says, “This is a list of the largest farms by revenue, with every owner's contact information and address on it. It also has the contact information of the political officials who hold Council seats with the ICO.”

Vinny laughs and slaps Sal on the back. “My number two guy is always pulling through. When he first showed me this I almost shat my pants. Great, great work, Sal.”

Joe stares coldly at Sal as he sees his father praise the Underboss. The man who does not share in the DiGrasso name. The man who has no right to take over as the Don when Vinny steps down. Joe asks, “What about the language barrier? Are we going to need a Vietnamese translator? And what happens if we attend one of these Council meetings? Are we going to need a translator for every country represented?”

Sal replies “Luckily the Council has considered this problem, and has agreed that everyone speaks a common language at the meetings. All members must speak English at the meetings, or have an English translator.”

Everyone at the table rolls their eyes. “Ugh, English is such an ugly language!” remarked Tony. “We can’t force them to speak Italian like us? Listen to this, It’s a beautiful language.” Everyone at the table laughs.

Sal replies, “Unfortunately, no. We cannot, Tony. And to answer the rest of your question, Joe. We will need a translator for the negotiations with the farmers. I have a hard time believing they will speak Italian or English very well.”

“Great,” remarks Joe. “I have a guy we can trust. I’ll give him a call tomorrow.”

“No need,” replied Sal. “I already called a translator who will be helping us.”

Joe looks at Vinny, then back at Sal. Joe says, “I mean, that’s great, Sal, but I need someone I can trust. I'm not going to be working with some rando I've never met before."

Vinny replies, "Giuseppe. Rest assured. Sal wouldn't call a guy who is untrustworthy. Right, Sal?"

"That's right, Vin," Sal retorts.

Another moment of silence passes. Then, Gio speaks up. "So, are all six of us moving to Vietnam for a while until we finish the plan? It sounds kinda complex. Would we have to be living there for a few years?"

Sal answers, "Vinny will stay here in Sicily. As the Don, you are never expected to do the dirty work. I'll be overseeing the operation in Vietnam, Joe and Tony will be implementing the high-level strategy and communications, and you two will be doing entry-level work. Gotta start somewhere. As for the timing, well, the Council meets every six months, and I can't imagine we would need more than two meetings to… influence the Council members to implement our proposed regulations. In regards to buying the farms, that should be quick. I don't think it will take more than a month. We're going to give them offers they can't refuse. It's easy to make big bets on an investment when you control the outcome."

Nick cuts in, "So we might have to live there for the next year?"

"Well," said Sal. "I'll be with you." He points to Tony and Joe, "These guys will be with you. And of course, the five of us will be making trips back to Sicily frequently."

Another moment of silence passes. Gio breaks this silence and exclaims, "Cool! Sounds like a good opportunity. I've never been to Vietnam." He turns to Vinny and says, "Mr. DiGrasso, thank you for the trust and opportunity to prove my loyalty. I think you'll find there are no young adults in Italy who will work harder than me or Nick."

Tony scoffs at this.

Vinny hits the table with his palm. "I love this kid's energy!" he exclaimed. Then Vinny holds up his wine glass and adds, "Welcome to the business, kid."

As the empty bottles of Chianti start piling up on the kitchen table, the mood shifts more light-hearted. Nick and Gio are back to their poking fun at each other; most of the jokes are about Gio's fedora. Tony and Joe spend time getting to know the younger soldiers. Vinny and Sal are mostly watching all of this unfold, with smiles on their faces, adding commentary here and there.

Nobody had a clue that by the end of this operation, two people at this table would be gone forever.

Dinner, drinking, and joking eventually come to an end. Nick stands up, thanks Vinny for hosting them at his lovely home, and says, "Let's go Gio. Sofia is expecting me back soon."

"Is Sofia your wife, Nick?" asked Joe.

"Nah, girlfriend," he replied. "We got a little apartment in the city."

"You, your girl, and your brother?" asked Tony.

Nick laughs. "No, no. Sofia and I live together," he says. Then he points to Gio and adds,

"This one thought it'd be fun to rent the apartment right next door to us because he has separation anxiety. And he figured since we live close, I'll drive his ass everywhere."

Gio shrugs. "I'm the best neighbor you could ask for," he said, grinning.

Joe gets up and says, "Yeah Tone, let's go. I gotta get back to Jo."

Gio looks at Joe confused and says, "Aren't you Joe?" Joe replies, no my wife's name is Josephine, so it's J-O, Jo. I'm J-O-E, Joe."

"That's confusing," said Gio.

Tony laughs at this.

"Yeah yeah," said Joe. "Let's go, Tone."

Sal turns to Vinny and says, "Hey Vin, you mind if I stay a little longer? It's been a little too quiet at the house since Teresa passed."

Vinny grabs Sal's shoulder and gives him a look of consolation. "Of course, Sal. Stay as long as you need."

Joe and Tony walk out of the house in unison with Nick and Gio. Tony and Joe walk towards the red ‘62 Alfa Romeo.

Nick gawks at the car. “Whoa,” he said. “Is that your car?”

“Yeah,” replied Joe. “It’s nice, eh? It’s important to have a status symbol when you finally reach a high status.”

Nick looks at the Alfa Romeo, back at his black 2019 Fiat 500, and back at the Romeo, stunned. While he is gawking, Tony and Joe slide into the car and drive off.

3

Joe drops off Tony at his apartment and heads home. It’s about 11:30 pm when he walks into the kitchen through the garage. He hears the television on in the living room and goes to investigate. He sees Josephine on the couch with a glass of red wine, watching a tennis match on the TV. “Ah, watching some tape, eh?” he asked.

She turns her head, sees him, and smiles. “It’s important to watch yourself so you can improve on your weaknesses.”

Joe replies, "Oh you have no weaknesses, baby.”

“Everyone has weaknesses,” she replied.

Joe sits next to her. “I have some pretty big news,” he said.

With her attention still on the television, Josephine asks, “What news, baby?”

“I’m gonna have to go away for some time,” he said.

Josephine turns her head to Joe, questioningly.

He adds, “I can explain more later, but the family is buying a few coffee farms in Vietnam. Me, Tony, Sal, Nick, and Gio are gonna have to go over there to see the purchases and investments through.”

“Who are Nick and Gio?” she asks.

Joe answers, “Sal’s kids. Big mistake gettin’ them involved if you ask me, but they are nice enough to have around.”

Josephine nods. “How long will you be gone?”

Joe says, “Could be just a few months. Worst case scenario would be around a year.” There is a moment of silence, and Josephine nods along, processing the information. Then, she breaks the silence. “Well… if you have to go, you have to go. We have nannies for the kids, and I’ll keep busy with Tennis. You’ll be able to visit while you’re gone though, right?”

Joe nods. “Of course, baby,” he said.

The two embrace in a hug. Josephine adds, “Well, I’ll of course miss you, but if you gotta do it for the family, you know you have my support.”

Joe leans in and puts Josephine's soft, gentle lips to his own. “When do you leave?” she asked.

“Sounds like we leave in a month,” he said.

“Well, we’ll just have to make the most out of this month then, huh?” she said. This time, she leans in for a kiss. Josephine reaches for the remote and turns off the television. She then reaches for Joe’s hand, pulls him off the couch, and they head upstairs to their room together to make love.

4

Meanwhile, Nick and Gio arrive at their apartment building. They park and step out of the tiny Fiat. They walk through the dim parking garage, and up the stairs to their apartment. “Wanna hang out for a little? It’s still pretty early," said Gio.

Nick replies, “Yeah, sure. You can chill with Sof and me for a little bit. But not too late. If we only have a month left in Sicily, Sofia and I are gonna have to make the most of our short time left together if you know what I mean.”

Gio says, “Yeah don’t worry. I don’t wanna be anywhere near you two for that.”

Nick chuckles and opens the door to his apartment.

The two boys step into the apartment. It is a modest-sized one-bedroom apartment. The place is kept neat, and has a candle perpetually burning in the kitchen with the scent of ‘Sicilian Lemon’. It is an open floor plan so the kitchen opens up to the living room, making it all feel like one big room. Once they step in, they are immediately greeted by Sofia.

Sofia DiaMatto is a tall thin woman with shiny black hair, a dark olive skin complexion, and deep brown eyes. She is the daughter of two well-known authors. Her father, Luigi DiaMatto wrote a travel book in his twenties that became a worldwide hit. He traveled a great deal as a kid since his father, Sofia's grandpop, was in the Italian army. He wrote about traveling the world, and the strange things he experienced as a mere boy. Her mother, Francesca DiaMatto became known from her novel, *The Road Ahead,* a tale of two Italian soldiers who were best friends, drafted into the war together, and then struggled to fit into society once they came home from ten years of service. The book was actually about her father and his best friend. This novel was also the true story of how Francesca and Luigi, Sofia's parents, met. Luigi's father was Francesca's father's best friend. They would hang out all the time, sharing war stories, and drinking excessive amounts of brandy and espresso. When they would hang out, they would bring their kids to have playdates. Once the kids were older, the playdates stopped, but only because the real dates started. They quickly fell in love, got married, and had a baby girl they named Sofia DiaMatto.

Growing up, Sofia felt a great deal of pressure to become a writer. Not because her parents pushed her in that direction, but because *both* of her parents were famous authors. She would get frustrated with her writings though because she never thought they were any good. "Write about your *experiences*," her parents used to tell her. Easy for them to say. They have the most romantic love story of all time and had the opportunity to experience the world as children. Sofia always felt a little jealous of their experience. Resented it, even. How was she supposed to become a world-renowned author if she wasn't provided the same real-life experiences her parents were?

As she grew older, she met Nick Conti – a boy who made her feel *alive*. They always had a rush together. He would take her to the beach for sunsets, they would hit the town together and get in trouble. Never serious trouble, just fun, memorable trouble. She especially loved him because he supported her dream of becoming a writer. He would tell her she is going to make it big one day – he just *knew* it. Sofia knew right away she wanted to marry this man one day. But that story is yet to come.

When the boys enter, she greets them with, "Hey boys, how was dinner?"

Gio replies, "Hey Sofia. It was good! Lots of good food and good wine."

Nick walks over to her and kisses her lips. "Yeah, Vinny busted out some old vintage Chianti he had in his cellar. When we start making more money we gotta get a cellar and fill it with wine and shit," he said.

"I like the sound of that," said Sofia, smiling.

"I do have some important news though," said Nick. All three of them sit on the white, plush couch in the living room.

Gio looks down at the floor. He thought Nick would wait until the couple was alone to tell her about Vietnam.

"The new venture requires us to be gone for some time," Nick said, pointing to himself and Gio.

"Oh?" she said, intrigued. "Where to? And how long is 'some time'?"

Nick sighs and says, "We're going to Vietnam. It could be a few months, it could be an entire year. Worst case is a year though."

Sofia looks a little shocked, but the glimmer in her eyes shows possible excitement. "Wow, that sounds like a big assignment. I'm obviously going to miss you, but this sounds like a great opportunity for you boys! Does this mean you are stepping up your responsibilities in the family?"

Nick says, "Yeah, it definitely sounds like it. It is just me, Gio, our Pops, and Vinny's two sons, Joe and Tony. It seems like we'll have a big role in this operation."

Sofia's smile grows from ear to ear. She hugs Nick and says, "Congrats baby! That's incredible.

All your hard work is paying off." She turns to Gio and hugs him as well. "You boys deserve this! Hopefully, it is only a few months though. I'm gonna miss you boys."

"We'll miss you too," said Gio.

Then Nick says, "Yeah, we'll really miss you. But it sounds like we'll be able to make plenty of trips back home. Shit, maybe you can even visit. We can make a trip out of it."

She smiles again and replies, "Ooooooh, I've never been to Vietnam! Maybe it'll be just the inspiration I need to start a new book. I've been wanting to write about traveling and experiencing other countries, but my professors – and of course parents – say it's important to write about things you know, and well… I've never left Italy."

Nick smiles and says, "Yeah, maybe babe."

Sofia jumps off the couch and onto her feet. "Well, what do you boys say we keep this party going? Big news is cause for a big celebration!" She runs over to the kitchen, pulls a bottle of champagne out of the fridge, and grabs three glasses from the cabinet.

Nick and Gio stand up. “I’m down!” says Gio and runs over to the kitchen.

“Yeah, me too,” Nick said, smiling and walking over to them. The three of them spend the rest of the night celebrating, and drinking champagne – completely unaware that the journey they are about to embark on will change the course of their young lives.

Chapter 3

Nam Le

A month passes, and the mid-morning July sun in Sicily is blazing on. Joe and Tony are sitting next to each other in first class on a Boeing 777, which is still on the ground at the Catania airport. Final destination – Ho Chi Minh City, Vietnam.

Tony turns to the window seat towards Joe and says, “I’m sweatin’ my dick off, Joe. Is Vietnam gonna be this hot? I hope our hotel has a pool.”

Joe is reading a book called 'The Ins and Outs of Coffee Farming'. He keeps his focus on the book and distractedly answers, "Yeah Tone, I'm sure that place is hot as hell in July."

Nick and Gio are sitting in the row behind them, and Sal has a row to himself, ahead of Joe and Tony. Gio is wearing a neck pillow and over-ear headphones and is crushing his second mimosa. Nick looks at Gio, appalled.

"Hey man, you look ridiculous. We're on a business trip. Act like you've done this before," he said.

Gio turns to him and worriedly replies, "Is this a bad look? Is it the Mimosa? Should I not be drinking on a business trip?"

"Gio, it's all of it. Take that fucking pillow off and stop slamming that Mimosa. Just act like you've been in first class is all. Appearance is a big part of this job if you want to be taken seriously."

Gio takes the neck pillow off and slows down on the Mimosa.

Finally, the plane starts moving. Five minutes later, the men are in the air, about to begin the most harrowing journey of their careers.

1

Many hours and one layover in Dubai later, they arrived. It is eight o'clock in the morning when they touch down in Ho Chi Minh City. Once the plane lands, Sal stands to get his carry-on and turns to face the four men sitting behind him.

He says, "Alright guys, listen up. Our translator, Binh Nguyen, will be waiting for us outside the airport. He's taking us to our hotel. We will have four hours to get checked in, and meet Nam Le at the first farm."

"Who is Nam Le?" asked Tony.

Nam Le was the son of a coffee crop farmer, who was the son of a rice paddy farmer. Nam's grandfather Minh, worked long hard hours in the rice paddies. He worked until his body would give up on him, almost daily. Being a single father of six kids, that is what he had to do to make ends meet. His wife, Nam's grandmother, passed away immediately after birthing her sixth child, due to complications from the birth. Nam's father, Duong, had conflict with Minh. At sixteen years old, Duong would take beatings from his father when he'd said he didn't want to work sixteen hours on the rice paddies during the weekends. He would complain about how Saturdays and Sundays were the only days he had a break from school, and he just wanted to rest. Minh would beat and scold him, saying it was Duong's responsibility as the eldest child to set an example. "Working hard is admirable," Minh used to tell Duong. "It is the sign of a man who is able to provide." This would drive Duong crazy. He used to tell Minh that he works sixteen hours a day, seven days a week, and he *still* can't provide for his family. "It's not about how hard you work, it's about what you *do* for work," he used to retort back to Minh. One day, while Duong was getting scolded by his father for the usual shit, he used this retort, but added "and what *you* do is *useless*!" He immediately regretted saying that and took the worst beating of his life just seconds later.

Finally, when Duong was ready to move out and start a family of his own, he promised to *do* something valuable for work. If he was working sixteen hours a day, it better be because he damn well wanted to. *Not* because he had to.

Duong loved to read, and one day he was reading an article about how his home country, Vietnam is one of the fastest-growing coffee-exporting countries in the world. The article cited the climate and geography as near-perfect conditions to grow the crop, specifically the Robusta bean. *Perfect*, he thought. *This is the perfect opportunity to get in on the ground floor!* "Soon to be Vietnam's largest export. Possibly to become the largest coffee exporting nation in the world," he read aloud himself. The only problem was that it cost a gobsmacking amount of money to purchase the amount of land necessary to start a coffee farm. And money was something Duong lacked greatly as a new father and struggling restaurateur.

Just two days after reading that article, Duong found out his father, Minh had passed away.

He had a mix of emotions. He was generally sad since Minh was his father, but even in his sorrow, he just kept thinking about the beatings he used to take. Those nasty, brutal beatings. When he thought about the whoopings, he felt less sad about his father passing. However, he also hated thinking about the beatings. It was a lose-lose.

Shortly after discovering his father passed, he received good news about something else, which helped him learn that sometimes great news can come out of bad news. Like a sadistic Matryoshka stacking doll set. One doll is hidden in the next.

The good news was that Minh left him one hundred percent of the rice paddy in his will, stating that as the oldest child, it was Duong's duty to run the family business – keep it alive. But Duong was no schmuck. He didn't want the life his father had; therefore, he sold the rice paddy. *It's about what you do for work*, he kept reminding himself. This mantra, and the article about Vietnamese coffee, inspired him to use the money from the rice paddy for a down payment on a big plot of land, to begin his new journey as a coffee farmer. His goal: own the largest coffee farm in all of Vietnam by export volume, and landmass.

He eventually went on to achieve this goal.

When Duong got the farm up and running, it was an instant success, generating more revenue than any other farm in Vietnam within its first two years. The business and the coffee industry were booming. Duong used to take his only child, a boy by the name of Nam, to the farm with him in the summers. Nam would ride on the back of the four-wheeler, grasping onto his father's waist as if they were going two hundred miles an hour. They would watch the sunset over the rolling green landscape with Nam's mother. Nam would pick coffee cherries off the bushes and eat them raw, consuming the whole fruit and both raw coffee beans inside it. He made some of his best childhood memories on that farm.

As time went on, both Nam's parents became ill, but at different times. It was his mother who passed away first. His parents were heavy smokers early in his childhood. He has memories of his mother going through a pack of cigarettes before lunch. She developed lung cancer first. It was a brutal sight. She was coughing and spitting up blood constantly. Even would lose her voice so seriously she couldn't speak for days at a time. She suffered through that for about eight months until she passed. It was so hard to watch, that Nam's father went cold turkey within the first week she was diagnosed. He didn't touch a cigarette for the remainder of his life. Unfortunately, he made that decision too late. Just two years after Nam's mother passed, his father Duong passed away as well, leaving Nam an orphan at eighteen years old.

When Duong was near the end of his life, he made sure to put Nam in his will to receive the coffee farm empire he built from the rice paddy money. Duong used to tell Nam about his struggles growing up. How his father would beat him, insult him, and scold him for not wanting to work in the rice paddies. He'd tell Nam how he built the coffee farm from the ground up. Nam thought his father was invincible. The smartest man on earth. Those evenings when Nam and both of his parents would sit on the grass, and watch the sunset over the luscious green mountains were transformative. Those moments inspired him to carry on his father's legacy that he worked so hard to create. In Nam Le's eyes, if he could carry on his legacy, he would never truly be gone.

That is the correct answer to Tony's question "Who is Nam Le?"

But of course, none of the Sicilians knew Nam's backstory, so Sal simply replied, "he's the first coffee farmer we're meetin' with. I want us to start negotiations today. We'll meet with the second farmer tomorrow. We'll see how those negotiations go, and decide who else to reach out to if needed."

"Why the rush, Sal?" asked Joe.

"Because the ICO meeting is in September. That means we only have two months to make our investments. Except for that, we need to catch the attention of the ICO members in Hanoi and influence them to push our agenda. That will take most of our time over the next two months, so really I'd say we only have about two weeks to make our investments."

Gio turns pale upon hearing all this information. He was excited about what is to come at the beginning of the plane ride, but now that they are in Vietnam and the talk is getting real, his nerves begin taking over. He turns to Nick who seems cool as a cucumber, taking in this information. "I'm gettin' nervous, Nick. Are you nervous? Even a little?"

"Fuckin' terrified," he replied. Nick turns to face Gio and says, "But this is *our* time."

2

The five men walk off the plane and grab their luggage from baggage claim. As promised, Binh Nguyen, a short Vietnamese man with jet-black hair and dark eyes, is waiting for them outside in a black Escalade. The car sticks out like a sore thumb as all the other vehicles swerving in and out of the airport lanes are compact cars or motorcycles. "Jesus, Sal," said Joe. "Couldn't he have picked a car that fits in a little better around here?"

Sal points to a compact car driving on the tight, airport road lanes and responds, “You think we all could’ve fit in one of those tiny ass cars? I don’t think so.”

Joe sighs and walks towards the car along with the rest of the guys. Under his breath, Joe murmurs to Tony, “I already don’t trust this guy.”

Tony doesn’t reply, but his face hardens.

Binh opens the hatchback of the Escalade, and the guys throw their luggage inside. Then, they pile inside, with Sal taking the passenger's seat. “Binh!” exclaimed Sal. “It’s been years. How are you, my old friend?”

Binh, with only a light Vietnamese accent, replies, “I’ve been great, Sal! How have you been?”

“Can’t complain, can’t complain.” Sal points to the back of the vehicle. “These are my two boys, Nicholas, and Giovanni. And in the far back row, those are Vinny’s boys. Anthony, and Giuseppe.”

Binh greets the four guys with a smile. “Pleased to meet you all.” They all greet him back in unison.

Binh begins driving away from the airport, when Joe asks, "Hey so uh, Binh. How does a Vietnamese guy like yourself know Italian?"

"Good question," Binh replied. My father and Sal's father worked closely together when the Cosa Nostra had their strong presence in the Heroin distribution here in Vietnam. My father was Sal's father's main contact. Of course, my father had to know Italian for this to work. The language was so beautiful to me, I just had to learn it. As a child, I would beg my father to take me on his work trips to Sicily, so I could see the culture and hear the language. After months of pleading, he gave in and started taking me along. I learned the language by being immersed in your beautiful culture and hearing the elegant sounds of Sicily. That is also how I met Sal. We used to play as our fathers would discuss business."

"Huh, interesting," replied Joe.

For the next hour, the guys sit in silence in the gargantuan black Escalade. They are all taking in all the sites, smells, and sounds of their new home for the foreseeable future. All of them are stunned by the scale of Ho Chi Minh City. They had no idea how developed it was. Then again, they never thought about it. Finally, they arrive at the hotel. All the guys get checked in and unload their luggage in their rooms. Nick and Gio are rooming together, as are Tony and Joe, and Binh and Sal.

3

In Gio and Nick's room, Gio lays down on his bed, looking up at the ceiling – his fedora covering his face. It feels as though someone is twisting Gio's stomach like a sadistic Rubik's Cube.

Nick raises an eyebrow and says, "Gio, you look like an American Cowboy. Something wrong?"

"Just nervous is all," he answered.

Nick's voice turns serious and he says, "Just remember, this is *our* time. Our time to prove our loyalty. Our time to show we can do good work. And most importantly, our time to secure a good spot in the family."

Gio sits upright and puts the fedora back on his head. “You’re right,” he said. “No time to bitch and moan. We gotta make names for ourselves.”

4

Meanwhile, in Tony and Joe’s room, Tony is already asleep on his bed. Joe stands up from leaning over his suitcase and sees Tony fast asleep. Joe picks up his shoe and throws it at Tony, hitting him in the stomach. Tony shoots upright.

“Ow! What the fuck, Joe?”

“How can you be asleep already? We got a lotta shit to take care of today, Tone!” he replied.

“I’m just so tired!” said Tony. “You know I can't sleep on public transportation. This is why I hate traveling. The first couple of days I’m tired and grumpy.”

Joe scolds, “I don’t think it is just when you’re traveling, jackass.”

“Whatever. If I’m not as sharp as usual, you know why,” said Tony.

Joe answers, ”Don't make excuses, Tone. We got business to take care of. No time for excuses.”

5

Ten minutes later, all 6 of them meet in the hotel lobby. "You boys ready?" asked Sal.

"You bet, Sal," replied Joe. "Let's go make an offer they can't refuse."

Sal looks to his sons. He sees Gio's typical olive complexion, now pale as milk. "Gio, everything okay?" he asked.

"Yeah, Dad. Everything's great!" he said, unconfidently. Binh grabs the keys out of his pocket and shakes them in the air. "Shall we?" he asked, and the men walked toward the black Escalade.

In the car, Sal briefs the guys. "This farm is 45 minutes away from the hotel. As I said before, we'll be meeting with a man named Nam Le. He owns and operates the largest farm in Vietnam in both acreage and revenue. He's been running this farm his entire adult life, and apparently, it has a family history, so it is unlikely he will want to sell right away. But again, our game plan is to make an offer at market price, and if he refuses, we up the offer to a point he can't refuse. Capiche?"

The guys reply in unison. “Capiche,” they said.

“Good,” said Sal. He then pulls out a suitcase from the floorboard.

“Now, everyone take one for protection.” He passes the suitcase back to Nick, who opens the suitcase. It is chock-full of all types of pistols. The suitcase gets passed around until everyone in the car has a piece. The rest of the car ride is spent in silence, as their minds wander like a lost boat at sea. Wondering about the unknown that lies ahead of them. Wondering how much time they will spend on this new planet.

6

Finally, they arrive at the first farm in Vietnam. They are driving through a thick jungle environment – nothing like their drive through the highly populated and urban Ho Chi Minh City. The men in the car are only able to see the dirt road ahead of them. The trees surrounding the vehicle are so dense, it is like trying to see the ocean floor miles beneath you. Nothing but darkness. This certainly doesn't help Gio's stomach. In fact, he feels the knots tightening even more.

As they progress through the bumpy, winding dirt road, the trees begin to open up. The landscape becomes conceivable to the visitors. The guys in the black Escalade are awestruck. They find themselves driving through beautiful, mountainous terrain – lush, and covered in greenery. The mountains feel as though they are alive. As if they have a breath of their own – a soul.

Tony is the first to break the silence. "Holy fuckin' shit," he remarked. "This place is gorgeous!"

Binh laughs and says, "Yes, yes. The terrain here in Vietnam is quite diverse. There are not many places on earth where you have a large urban area like Ho Chi Minh City, and then lush, green mountains within an hour of each other. But I must forewarn you, these mountains are like Sea Sirens. They draw you in with their beauty, only to bring destruction. Stay alert."

Nick asks, "What do you mean by that? Like, watch out for animals?"

"Perhaps," replied Binh. "But watch your sanity as well."

This statement turns Gio's stomach into a spider web of knots.

They pull up to a small shack made of brick. It doesn't seem to be the most stable structure of all time, but there is a sensation radiating from it. One of great power.

Binh steps out of the car first, and the remainder follows. "You think this guy speaks English? Or any off chance he speaks Italian? If not, we're gonna make you earn your wage early on, huh?" asked Sal.

"No telling," replied Binh. "Only one way to find out." They step into the little shack, and see a small man with dark skin, darker eyes, and even darker hair, sitting at a desk made of plywood. He turns to them as they step inside, and speaks a few sentences in Vietnamese quickly and excitedly.

Sal breaks out his English for the first time in years and asks the proprietor of the farm, "Uh, hey there. Do you speak English? Or maybe Italian?"

Nam Le smiles at Sal and replies, "Un poco."

Tony looks at Joe, confused, and says, "What the fu– is that fucking Spanish?"

Sal turns to Binh and asks, "Can you just tell me what he said when we initially walked in?"

Binh tells the Sicilians, "He said, 'Welcome! I am Nam Le, and this is my empire. Nice to finally meet you!'"

Sal nods at Binh, turns to Nam Le, and says, "Thank you for meeting with us, Mr. Le. My name is Sal Conti. This here is Anthony, Giuseppe, and my two sons, Nicholas and Giovanni. I don't want to take up too much of your time so I'll cut to the chase."

Binh is hurriedly translating this to Nam Le. "We would like to purchase your magnificent land here. Our Company would like to expand into the coffee industry, and what better place than this?"

Binh finishes up translating this to Nam. Nam's face hardens, and replies in Vietnamese with a change of tone.

Binh translates, "He thought you were coming here for a tour of the farm like the other tourists typically do. He wants to know what price you would be willing to pay for the farm he spent his whole life cultivating."

Sal pulls a pen out of his breast pocket, points to a legal pad on Nam Le's desk, and asks, "May I?" Nam Le rips a page out of the legal pad and hands it to Sal. Sal writes a number on the page and shows it to the rest of the Sicilians. Joe nods in agreement, and Sal hands the paper over to Nam Le.

The second Nam sees what is written on the paper, he scoffs a few curse words in Vietnamese and rips the paper in half. He then stares at Sal, insulted, and spits on the ground in front of Sal's feet. This lights a fire in Tony's belly. Nobody disgraces the family like that. Even if that person is ole' uptight ass, Sal.

Tony picks up the paper, shakes it in front of Nam's face, and yells, "HEY! The fuck you spittin' at us for, eh?! Where is your respect?! You don't wanna be on our bad side, pal!"

Joe pulls Tony back by the shoulders and gives him a look that says, 'Cool it down.'

Once Tony settles down, Sal points again to the legal pad. Nam hesitantly rips another piece off the pad, and hands it to Sal. He once again writes a number down and hands it to Nam Le. Without hesitation, Nam Le rips the paper up a second time.

Infuriated, Sal yells, "Okay now what the fuck! That offer is five times the market value of this farm. What could you possibly want?!"

Binh translates this in a more calm tone to Nam. Binh translates back to Sal, "He said he wants to know why you want the farm so bad before he sells. He said if you're willing to spend so much on his land, there must be a reason for it, and he wants to know that reason before he sells. He is skeptical why someone who hasn't even walked the land or knows anything about coffee farming is interested in paying so much for it."

"You don't need to know, pal," said Sal. "I'm offering FIVE TIMES what this shithole is worth. Don't make a mistake now!"

Binh translates this to Nam. Nam looks at Sal who is now red in the face and shaking. He begins laughing at Sal's red face.

To this, Sal replies, "You can take our generous offer, or we will *make* you take our offer."

Nam, making the biggest mistake of his life, miscalculates Italian rage. He imagines Sal's face turning into a red, plump Italian tomato. He laughs even harder at this, almost falling out of his chair.

Tony begins fuming. *He's laughing at the Family*, he thinks.

Nam is now cackling uncontrollably. Tony pulls out a Colt .45 from the waist of his pants and shoots Nam squarely between the eyes. The room that once was filled with maniacal laughter is quickly filled with an ear-shattering crack, and then dead silence. Then another sound fills the shack. Joe, Tony, Sal, and Nick turn around to see what the wretched sound is. It is Gio vomiting in the back corner. The knots in his stomach have officially taken over as he loses his breakfast. Good thing they haven't eaten lunch yet.

Joe and Sal turn wide-eyed and face Tony. He is standing still, stone-faced, looking at Nam's limp body on the ground. Smoke from the gun is spilling out of the barrel, and dancing up towards the ceiling as if trying to escape the scene. Blood and brain matter ooze slowly and hesitantly out of the small hole in Nam's head. Gio, who is already at ground level on all fours, looks up, sees the obscenity that was once Nam Le's head and vomits again. Nick runs over to comfort Gio while Joe and Sal stay staring at Tony, in disbelief.

"What the fuck, Tone!" yelled Joe. "We haven't been here for a full twenty-four hours and you already put us in a situation like this?! What happened to cleaning up your act, huh?! What happened to no more sloppy work?!"

Tony replies, "He deserved it, Joe! We can't let people disrespect us like that!"

Sal cuts in and says, "How can you say he deserved it? You met him for two goddamn seconds!"

Meanwhile, Gio is able to gather himself and stand upright. Nick walks back to the group with him slowly.

Tony hears them walking, turns around towards them, and points in the direction saying, “At least I’m not throwin’ up in the middle of a business meetin’.”

Sal heatedly replies, “He didn’t throw up in the middle of a business meeting. He threw up when your thick skull *ended* the business meeting with a bullet!”

Joe, Tony, and Sal begin shouting at each other in unison. After a couple of seconds, Nick cuts in.

“GUYS! All this arguing is helpin’ nobody. Tony, it was a bad move shootin’ Mr. Le, but hey, now we get the farm for free, right?”

“Wrong,” said Joe. “We need the ICO council member to know we own this farm, and all the other farms we purchase, so they realize we have power. It’ll be much harder for them to disagree with us if they know we control the largest percentage of market share in their coffee economy. We still need to buy it."

Sal continues this thought, saying, "Yes. And if we don't execute a proper, legal transaction, the farm could go to Nam's next of kin, or worse, be seized by the government. We don't want this to turn into a bigger headache than it already is."

Gio, is feeling better enough to start thinking clearly, and asks, "How can we execute a legal transaction of the farm if Nam is dead though?"

"Well," said Sal, "we're going to need to draft up some paperwork for a transaction and make it seem legit. In the meantime, we need to get rid of his body and make sure nobody figures out what happened before the paperwork goes through."

Joe runs over to the desk that Nam Le was once sitting at, and begins rummaging through the cabinets.

He says, "We will need some sort of personal identification and business incorporation letters for the paperwork to go through properly." Joe tries to open the last drawer in the desk on the bottom left, but it is locked shut. He jimmies the drawer a few times, but it refuses to open.

"Shit. It's locked," he said.

Gio walks over to where Joe is leaning over the desk. He picks up a paperclip that was on Nam's desk and unfolds it. He steps in front of Joe and jams the unfolded paperclip into the lock of the drawer. After about 15 seconds of jimmying the lock, it pops open. Joe stands there, looking at Gio, flabbergasted. Gio then rummages through the last drawer and pulls out a Vietnamese passport, and papers that appear to be Articles of Incorporation.

Gio smiles and in a small voice says, "I think we have us a sale."

Sal runs over to Gio, and slaps him on the back, laughing. "Great work, son!" he said.

Joe smiles, impressed, and says, "Yeah, great work, kid. We got us a sale. Now we need to figure out how we are going to operate this place in the meantime."

“What do you mean?” said Gio. “Doesn’t a place like this have workers who take care of operating it?”

“Yeah of course. But this place is a business. Someone needs to schedule workers, oversee the day-to-day operations, make payroll, and so on. And since we don’t have someone to do that dirty work for us anymore,” Joe said, glaring at Tony. “We'll need to find someone to take over those duties.”

Nick replies, “Yeah but we don’t know anyone in Vietnam except for Binh, and we need him to translate, not run some farm.”

Tony breaks his silence, and says, “Well we know of two people who are in Vietnam right now that could run this place.” With the gun still in his right hand, he points to Nick and Gio.

“No way!” said Nick. “We aren’t gonna run this place, that's not why we’re here.”

“You’re here to help the family where help is needed,” replied Tony. “Binh can’t run it, he is the translator. I’m the muscle. Joe and Sal are the brains.

You two are here for support. This is the support we need."

Gio hears this and throws up again, this time in front of the desk. Joe makes a squeamish face and steps away.

Sal cuts in and empathetically says, "Tony is right, Nicholas. You two are the soldiers, you're here for support. Besides, it won't be long. Just until Binh or someone else can introduce us to an individual who we can trust to run the farm. Two weeks, max."

Nick shoots back, "We've never operated a coffee farm! We won't even know what to do!"

Sal tries to console Nick, "You'll play it day by day. Deal with things as they come up. Besides, as I said, it'll be two weeks, max. Come on, you two are smart kids."

Tony scoffs at this.

Sal continues, "You can manage."

Nick, still infuriated, asks "Where will we stay? How are we going to get to the farm each day? We don't have a car!"

“I believe Nam lived on the farm. Didn’t you see the residence near where we parked?” replied Sal.

“No,” said Nick, gloomily.

“Again, two weeks max,” Sal answered.

Chapter 4

Lan Nguyen

Giovanni Conti's eyes flutter open as he awakens from a shitty night's sleep. The sunlight is already peering into the windows of the small house on the coffee farm he and Nick now call home. For the past two nights, sleep has eluded him. Eluded him the way a smooth criminal eludes the authorities. You want to catch the criminal.

You need to – but you can't.

Nightmares have been plaguing his sleep.

He has been haunted by something Binh said when they first arrived, while the other were gawking over the mountainous terrain. He thinks back to what was said.

"These mountains are like Sea Sirens. They draw you in with their beauty, only to bring destruction."

Then, when Nick asked, "What do you mean by that? Like, watch out for animals?"

Binh replied, "Perhaps, but watch your sanity as well."

Gio has been keeping a close eye on his sanity, but in doing so, feels like he is losing it.

He slides out of the tiny cot that is now his bed. He takes a deep breath and inhales the fresh mountain air that surrounds their new home. This air is the one thing that has kept Gio grounded for the past two days. That, and Nick's optimism. Ever since Nick accepted their new reality, he has been laser-focused on being the best damn coffee farm operator in the world.

Gio exhales a big breath, and walks out of the tiny room made of wood he and Nick share. As he enters the kitchen, he smells coffee and bacon. Nick is frying bacon on what appears to be a one-hundred-year-old stovetop, sipping coffee from a clay mug. Nick hears footsteps and without turning around greets him.

"Mornin' Gio. You get any better sleep last night?"

"Not really," he replied. "Still getting nightmares." Gio sits at the bar in the kitchen and sits on an unstable barstool.

Nick nods, unloads some bacon onto a plate in front of Gio, pours coffee into a mug near the plate and says, "Well, it should be another pretty chill day. The translator Binh got for us is already giving the workers their duties for the day. We just need to make the schedule for tomorrow and finish up some payroll stuff for this Friday."

Gio nods and chews his bacon. "Sounds good," he said. He becomes silent as his mind begins to drift to his summers in Sicily as a kid. Sal would take them to the beach. He and Nick would play one-on-one soccer in the sand.

Nick sees Gio's face turn blank as he seemingly glares into the abyss. He's worried about his younger brother, he's never seem him like this. Nick walks into the bathroom to get ready for the day, and Gio allows himself to be transported to that time of his boyhood. When things were simple. Just his two parents and partner in crime, Nick. After a while a slight, child-like smile sneaks up on his face as he reminisces.

1

Meanwhile Sal, Tony, Joe, and Binh are an hour south of what used to be Nam Le's pride and joy. They are already at the next farm on Sal's list. Binh is driving the black Escalade on another dirt road with stunning, mountainous terrain. Sal, who is sitting in the passenger seat, turns around to face Joe and Tony and says, "This next farm is the *second* largest in Vietnam. Between this one and the farm we currently own, we'll control about forty percent of the coffee exports in this country. That should be plenty to catch the attention of the ICO members. They'll probably reach out after this purchase to ask why three Sicilians who know nothing about coffee agriculture just bought the two largest coffee farms in their country. If not, that's okay. That's why we're going to Hanoi immediately after this purchase. Just in case."

"What's in Hanoi?" asked Tony.

Joe replies, "Hanoi is the Capital. It's where the government officials live and work."

"That's right," said Sal. "But again, we need this purchase to go through in order to really grab their attention." Sal looks Tony in the eyes. He says, pointedly, "That means every action we take in this negotiation will be methodic, and thoughtful. We are doing this one right. No shooting the proprietor of this farm, Tone. I don't care how much he makes fun of us. We need to swallow our pride here and get the job done. We got lucky the other deal went through so quickly without raising any eyebrows. This time, we aren't going to leave it to luck." Although, they will come to find that eyebrows were indeed raised.

Tony nods, stone-faced. “Loud and clear, Sal. Loud and clear.”

“Good,” Sal replied. “I had Binh preface the meeting with the fact that we are interested in a business deal, not just a tour. Learned our lesson on that one. Although, we do have a tour arranged. The owner, a gentleman by the name of Lan Nguyen, will be taking us around. I think we need to walk the farm this time around to show we are serious.”

“Agreed,” said Joe. “We should also go into this with a negotiation plan.”

“What exactly do you have in mind?” asked Sal.

“Well, Nam Le wasn’t keen on selling the farm to us. We need to be prepared for this… Lan Nguyen guy to deny an outright purchase as well.”

“Easy,” said Tony. “We tell him what happened to the first guy who turned down a purchase.”

“No!” said Sal. “I said we’re doing this one right. No mess.”

“I’m with you, Sal,” said Joe. “If he refuses, he offer a partnership. We let Lan continue running and operating the farm, and simply make an investment in his operation. No lower than fifty-one percent, of course, so we can retain control. And the majority of the prof–” Joe quickly turns his attention elsewhere. “Hey! What the hell you think you’re doin, Binh?!” Sal and Tony look in Binh’s direction and see him taking a long swig from a stainless steel flask.

“Binh,” said Sal pointedly. “I told you. Not while you’re working.” Without taking his eyes off the dirt road, Binh screws the top back on the flask and puts it in the console. Tony and Joe give each other a curious look.

“Joe, continue,” said Sal.

Joe does as he is bid. “And we can keep the majority of the profits this way.”

Tony asks, “Well, what if he doesn’t want to give up control?”

Joe replies, “Yeah, that’ll take some convincing. We will need to offer much more than what fifty-one percent of the farm is worth. Vinny cleared us to put in as much as eighty percent of the Farm's value, for only fifty-one percent control. But no more. That's should be a good enough deal"

"Isn't that considered a bad investment, Joe?" asked Tony.

"Nah Tone. Remember? This is essentially a riskless investment. When you take the risk out of this investment, it's worth a hell of a lot more than whatever eighty percent of the value is," said Joe.

Tony nods slowly, struggling to fully comprehend.

The Escalade pulls up to the estate on the farm. Binh exits the car. "No killin', right Tone?" said Sal.

"Yeah, Sal. No killin'."

The rest of the men exit the car. As they are walking toward a structure made of stone and brick, an off-roading safari-looking vehicle zips up between them and the structure. The driver was a small man with jet-black hair and black eyes. Binh and the

Sicilians stop quickly so as to not get hit by the vehicle.

He starts speaking in Vietnamese.

Binh translates, “He says, ‘Hello gentleman. My name is Lan Nguyen. Welcome to my farm.’”

Sal says, “Thank you, Lan. I’m Sal, this is Joe, Tony, and Binh, our translator.”

Binh translates this to Lan. Lan nods and in Vietnamese says, “Nice to meet you in person. Please, hop in the vehicle. We will take our tour now.” Binh translates this to the Sicilians.

Under his breath, Tony says to Joe, “We goin’ on fuckin’ safari or somethin’? Why does he have this eye-sore?”

Joe responds, quietly, “It’s a big fuckin’ farm, Tone. Probably can't walk around on foot very easily.”

The Sicilians enter the vehicle, and Lan takes off.

The ride is excruciatingly bumpy, especially because Lan is whipping the tall safari vehicle as if it is a go-kart.

"So," says Lan as Binh translates. "What interests you in coffee agriculture?"

Sal answers this, "We think there is a great opportunity in the market that our business and business partners can provide value to the industry as a whole."

He replies and Binh translates, "What value are you planning on providing that I haven't already provided, Mr. Conti? No offense, but I have twenty years of experience in this industry. How many years do you three have?"

They stop the vehicle at a line of what appears to be shrubs with red and green cherries growing on them. Lan hops out, and they all follow suit.

"Well," said Sal. "None in this particular industry, but we have a great deal of experience in other similar lines of work."

Binh translates this to Lan, and Lan gives Sal a condescending look. Lan replies in a haughty tone. Binh pauses, and the men look at Binh, waiting for a translation. Slowly and hesitantly, Binh provides the translation.

"Coffee isn't Heroin, Mr. Conti. You can't create a business model around people getting addicted to your product. You need the best crop. You need the know-how."

Tony turns to Joe and under his breath asks. "How'd he know we were Mafia?"

Joe shrugs.

Tony continues, "Seems a little racist to assume a couple of Sicilians are Mafia, doesn't it? I mean, if the Pope were here, would he assume the Pope is Mafia?"

Joe replies softly, "No, Tone, because the Pope ain't fuckin' Sicilian, dumbass. It's not racist. Don't get riled up."

Lan pulls one of the red cherries off a nearby shrub and asks something in Vietnamese.

Binh translates, "Did you even know that coffee beans grow inside these cherries? Do you know how many beans are growing in this cherry?

Do you know the varietal of this bean? Do you even know what a varietal is?"

Sal takes a beat, and then replies, "I do not, Mr. Nguyen. You're right. We need the know-how. That's why we are prepared to offer a tremendous price for your beautiful farm here and offer you a high-earning job as the operator of this enterprise."

Binh translates this and Lan scoffs. Binh translates as Lan is speaking quickly. "Why would I sell my ownership of this farm, and become an employee?"

Sal replies, "Owning a business is risky. Especially in the highly competitive coffee farming industry, as you well know. We are offered to assume that risk, and pay you a steady, above-market salary. No more seasonality in earnings, no more headaches with governmental paperwork, no more unknowns."

Lan walks toward another shrub, and looks at it fondly, thinking about Sal's words. Finally, he speaks up.

Binh translates, "Without risk, there is no reward. If we go into business, I still need to own a piece of the farm. I need the potential for a high reward."

Sal looks at Joe, who grins and shrugs. Joe steps forward, slaps Sal on the back, and says, "I'll take it from here, old man."

Joe looks at Lan. "We would like to offer a *partnership* in the venture, then."

Binh translates this to Lan, who appears interested.

Joe continues, "We are prepared to offer a… sizable investment, in exchange for fifty-one percent ownership of the farm. As you said before, we need you to operate the farm and provide the know-how, so you will still have the job as the operator, and with a good salary as well. Not as good as if we owned one hundred percent of the farm of course, but good nonetheless. Plus, you'll get a good chunk of change in this transaction because we're willing to pay well over market value."

Binh translates the rest of this proposal. Lan appears interested, but stays quiet. Lan breaks the silence.

Binh says, "He says he needs a minute to think."

Lan walks over to the vehicle and waves his hand for the men to get in as well. They all hop in, and Lan drives off.

The vehicle races through the mountains on the bumpy dirt road. The passengers sit silently, holding onto the vehicle so as to not fall out and break their necks. Joe is staring off into the distance, and sees a glimmer in his peripherals. He turns his gaze toward the inside of the vehicle, and sees the glimmer is coming from a stainless steel flask. Binh secretly took out the flask while the rest of the passengers were busy holding on for dear life and attempted a few quick swigs, most of which ended up on his shirt. Joe looks to Sal and Tony to see if they noticed this secret booze swig, but they are both looking out towards the mountains.

2

After about ten minutes, Lan parks the vehicle on the side of the dirt road. They are high on one of the mountains, surrounded by coffee cherry shrubs on either side of them. Directly in front of them is a beautiful overlook, with deep greenery expanding as far as the eye can see. In the lines of shrubs, there are workers with wooden and metal buckets at their feet. They are picking cherries swiftly and methodically, and tossing them in the buckets.

Lan steps out of the vehicle, and the Sicilians follow suit again. Lan walks over to a wooden fence in a clearing. Beyond the wooden fence, is a three thousand foot cliff. The five of them stand in a straight line, staring out into the beautiful, humbling view.

Lan speaks first. Binh translates, "Developed economies have taken advantage of emerging economies all throughout history. They have taken our land, depleted our resources, and screwed us out of what should be *our* profits. Why should I trust you men to be any different than what history has to show?"

Joe replies, "Because we'll be partners, Lan. In order for one of us to succeed, we both must. Our fifty-one percent ownership would be worthless if your forty-nine percent ownership was also worthless. We'll be in this together."

Binh translates this for Lan. Lan nods slowly, clearly deliberating these words. He turns around and points towards the workers, who are hurriedly picking the coffee cherries off the shrubs.

He replies in Vietnamese, "What about my workers? I can't run this farm without my workers."

Joe answers, "Then we'll keep them. Every last one of them. As I said, we'll leave you in charge of day-to-day operations, while we take care of the long-term and geopolitical strategy."

Lan turns back around to face the scenery. He takes another minute, deliberating on Joe's words. Finally, he turns to the Sicilians, smiles, and says something in Vietnamese.

Binh smiles and translates, "Sal, Joe, Tony. You have a deal!"

Sal smiles and reaches for Lan's hand to shake. "Thank you, Mr. Nguyen. We're excited to do business with you. And really – incredible work with this farm. I mean…" As Sal says this, he gestures towards the vast, gorgeous view past the wooden fence.

Lan shakes Sal's hand in return. He reaches for Joe's hand, then Tony's. Once all the handshaking is complete, they hop back into the safari vehicle and zip back to Lan's estate.

Once they reach the estate, they all exit the vehicle and stand between the black Escalade from which they drove in and Lan's house.

Sal reaches to shake Lan's hand again and says "Thanks again, My. Nguyen. We'll have our attorneys draft the offer papers and have them sent over for your signature."

Binh translates this to Lan, who smiles and nods in agreement. The rest of the men shake Lan's hand and then enter the Escalade.

"HELL YEAH!" exclaimed Tony once the doors were all shut. "Pop is gonna be blown away that we already have the two largest farms within our first week. We gotta celebrate back at the hotel."

Sal turns around to face Tony. “No time for celebration,” he said. “We’re going to Hanoi first thing tomorrow morning. But great job both of you. Really. You handled yourselves well, and we got the deal closed quickly. Let’s keep the quick, clean work going into Hanoi now.”

The black Escalade turns around and takes off, rocking on the dirt road like a sailboat at sea.

Joe asks “Sal, what do you think about trying to close a few more deals before going to Hanoi? I mean, we do only own two farms. Is that enough power to influence the ICO members?”

Sal replies, “Remember Joe. Those two farms control about forty percent of the nation's coffee exports. I’m certain they’ll be itchin’ to talk with us.”

After a moment of silence, Tony speaks up. “Damn, we should have asked Lan if he or anyone he knows can take over the day-to-day at Nick and Gio’s farm.”

Sal replies, “Let’s leave them be for now. They seem to be getting on just fine over there. I want us to lock down our proposed legislation with our soon-to-be friends in Hanoi first. One step at a time."

3

The next morning, Joe, Tony, Sal, and Binh are at the Ho Chi Minh airport, boarding their flight. Tony and Joe find their seats in first class. They are once again, in the row directly behind Sal.

Tony turns to Joe and says, "Goddamn, Joe. I don't know how much more flyin' I can take. Why are we flying, anyway? Wouldn't it be faster to drive? Vietnam can't be that big."

Joe replies, "It's a thirty hour drive, Tone. You think that would be better than a two hour flight?"

"Jesus Christ," Tony replied. "Well, let's stay in Hanoi for some time then. I just spent six months in a prison. I'd rather not be spending my time on the outside in a different prison with wings."

Joe smiles and opens a book to begin reading.

4

After two hours, the plane is flying over Hanoi, about to land. Tony and Joe are equally stunned at the beautiful, urban city. There are rivers running through the city. Bodies of water are encapsulated by it. The sheer size of Hanoi is striking to the brothers. They can't stop staring at the Red River or Ho Tay, also referred to as West Lake. It is a magnificent, yet daunting landscape. This reminds the brothers of the coffee farm visits. They are stunned by the gorgeous terrain, but at the same time, something feels off. The air, the water, the vibrant colors – something about it feels very foreboding.

5

The plane lands, and Binh and the Sicilians head to their hotel. When they are in the hotel lobby, Joe asks, "So Sal. When are we reaching out to these council members, eh? Shouldn't we have a few meetings lined up soon?"

Sal replies, "I called them this morning. As I predicted, they were itchin' to speak with us. We got a meeting lined up this evening."

Joe's face darkens. "When were you gonna tell us about this, Sal? Which council member?"

"We're meeting with both," said Sal. "And I was gonna tell you in a briefing over lunch. Relax, Joe."

"Well, it sure feels like you're tryna keep us in the dark. Do a lot of things yourself. The list of coffee farms, calling the council members," Joe turns and points to Binh, standing beside Sal. "Even this fuckin' guy! You got an alcoholic translator without any of us knowing. I don't know if I can trust this guy!"

Tony is standing still, watching Joe and Sal go at it, trying not to raise any more hairs than he already has.

Sal replies quietly, "Calm down, Giuseppe. We're in a lobby surrounded by people. I'm just doing my job as the Underboss. You understand. I'm not leaving any of you in the dark. If I was, I wouldn't take you to meet with the council members. But that's not the case now, is it?"

Joe's face reddens.

Tony cuts in and grabs Joe by the shoulders. He says, "Alright Joe let's go into the room and cool off, yeah?"

Joe allows himself to simmer down and walks into the elevator with Tony. Sal and Binh wait in the lobby for the next one.

Joe and Tony enter their hotel room, and Joe slams the door behind them, still fuming. "I gotta bad feelin' about that guy, Tone," he said.

Tony replies, "Who? Sal?"

"No!" said Joe. "Sal's alcoholic translator he calls a friend. That guy. He's gonna get us killed."

"I can get him killed before he gets us killed if that's what your gettin' at, Joe," said Tony.

Joe replies, "No, no, no. That will just make our problems worse. When we go back to Sicily, we need to tell Pops about this clown though. He's the only one who can reason with Sal and tell him it's time for a new translator."

Tony nods slowly. "When are we going back to Sicily?" he asked.

Joe lies down on the bed with his shoes still on. “Not sure, Tone. But hopefully sometime this month. I’m already missin’ Josephine and the girls.”

As he says this, Joe’s phone dings. He opens the notification to see his beautiful wife had sent him a selfie in her new tennis outfit, and his girls playing a match in the background on a court surrounded by palm trees. He sighs heavily.

Tony see’s a slight smile on Joe’s face, and then hears his longing sigh.

He asks, “What? The wife tempting you to come home with nudes or somethin’? Why the long face?”

Joe replies, “No, asshole. She sent me a picture of the girls playing tennis. I just miss them is all.”

“Well,” replied Tony. “At least you have people in your life to miss.”

Joe turns to him and says, “Well, you got me, Pops, Mom, and Nicolette.”

Tony lays down on his bed and replies, "Yeah, yeah, I know. I just wonder if it's too late for me to start a family of my own."

"It's not too late, Tone,"

Joe replied, empathetically. "It may never happen if you keep going to prison, but it's definitely not too late."

"Well, I don't wanna have to find my wife in prison. That is no place for women and children," Tony said, smiling. "But in all seriousness, thanks, Joe. It's nice having a pain-in-the-ass brother like you sometimes. You're uptight as hell, but you got some wisdom to share."

Joe smiles, still laying on the bed, looking up at the ceiling. "And your immature ass knows how to lighten the mood sometimes."

6

Meanwhile, in Sal and Binh's room, Sal's phone begins buzzing in his pocket. Nick is calling him. He accepts the call. "Hey boys!" said Sal. "How's everything going over at coffee paradise?"

"Good, Dad," said Nick. "Not too bad of work. We do all the scheduling, payroll, billing, and the translator helps us with all the client and accounts stuff."

"Good. I never had a doubt you guys would deliver results, though," Sal said. "How's Gio doing?"

Nick says, "Not amazing. He's been having nightmares and is constantly anxious – panic attacks even. It's not stopping him from getting shit done though."

Sal takes a beat and says, "Makes sense. This is a much more strenuous project than any of us had for our first job with the family."

Nick says, "Yeah, I'm sure."

They both fall silent for a moment. Eventually, Sal says, "Look after him, Nick. You know him best. If he's about to break, you let me know."

"Will do, Dad," he said. And they both hang up the phone.

At four-thirty that evening, all the men were cleaned up, and ready to meet the council members in one of the most important meetings of their lives. “You boys ready?” asked Sal.

“Yeah,” said Joe. “Time to win over some stiff necks.”

The four men walk out of the hotel and into the black Escalade. Twenty minutes later, the car pulls up in front of a three-story, white brick, square-shaped building. Sal, in the passenger seat, turns around to Joe and Tony and says, “Game time, boys.”

Chapter 5

The ICO

Tony, Joe, and Sal are waiting quietly in a small lobby to meet with the council members. Sal had Binh wait in the car. He felt comfortable leaving their prized translator for this meeting, since these two politicians spoke excellent English. They did, after all, receive plenty of practice speaking English at the ICO meetings, where it was the required language for all countries involved. Plus, Sal could smell Rice Wine on Binh's breath and didn't want any grief from Joe. Sal was worried the brothers had been catching on to some of Binh's, shall we say, heedless tendencies. Sal knew that after what Binh had gone through he became a drinker, but he wasn't aware of the severity of his issue. Sal was really worried about how long it had been since he and Binh saw each other. One could only imagine what other chaotic coping tendencies Binh picked up given what he went through. People have various methods of coping with trauma. Sometimes those methods just create more trauma rather than coping with it. It can be a vicious cycle, seemingly impossible to break. But if you find the right method, it is possible. Sal had a hunch Binh hadn't found one of the right methods yet.

The receptionist in the lobby who is sitting behind a desk, in front of two office doors answers a phone, nods, and quickly hangs up. She looks towards the Sicilians and in English says, "They are ready for you three."

Joe, Tony, and Sal nod and stand up. The receptionist gets up from her chair and opens the door to the left of her desk. She gestures for them to walk in.

As the three men walk in, they are greeted by a cloud of thick smoke. Sal walks in first and takes the biggest hit from the cloud. It smells of spicy tobacco, dung, and leather. Tony and Joe pile in behind Sal and are greeted with a lighter version of the same cloud. Although, it was still thick enough to make it feel like their eyebrows might burn off instantaneously.

They are greeted by two Vietnamese men. One is sitting behind a large mahogany desk, and the other is in a chair facing the desk. The one closest to them puts his hand out first. He greets them in English. "Gentlemen. A pleasure to meet you in person. I am Duc Pham."

Duc is an early thirties, short, stout man with jet-black hair and a devious smile.

"Duc, I am Sal. We spoke on the phone. This here is Giuseppe and Anthony DiGrasso."

As Joe shakes Duc's hand he says, "You can call me Joe."

As Tony shakes his hand he says, "And you can call me Tony."

While Duc shakes all their hands, the man behind the desk stands and introduces himself. "And I am Dong Tran."

Dong, still holding a cigar in one hand, shakes the hands of the strangers in his office with his free hand. Dong is a little older than Duc. He is in his early forties but looks to be damn near sixty. His wife tells him it is because of all the smoking, but he thinks it's probably the stress from when he served in the military. His once-black hair is now peppered with gray and his face appears to be made of leather. Not a fine Italian leather, but a cheaply made, dog-scratched leather. It reminds Sal of a couch his parents had when he was a mere boy. It was tough, rough, and ugly.

He hated that couch.

After the pleasantries are exchanged, everyone takes a seat. Dong sits behind his desk. Duc is in front of his desk, in a fold-out chair, and the three Sicilians find seats in the other fold-out chairs surrounding the desk alongside Duc.

"So, Mr. Conti," starts Dong. "What is it that you were hoping to discuss?"

"Well," Sal replies. "As I mentioned over the phone, we are very interested in the coffee industry as of late. So interested in fact, that we are now the owners of the two largest exporting coffee farms here in Vietnam. So I was hoping that we could chat – get to know each other. After all, we'll be in communication a great deal considering you two sit on the ICO Coffee Council as the Vietnam representatives. A country in which we now own about forty percent of the coffee exports."

Dong looks to Duc with what seems to be a fish hook caught in his eyebrow. "Is that so, Mr. Conti?"

Sal cuts in. "Please, just Sal."

Dong nods slowly, then replies, "Forty percent you say, Sal?"

"That's correct. Forty percent."

There is a moment of silence, as Duc and Dong appear to be communicating telepathically. "Well then, Sal. You say you would like to get to know each other. What is it you would like to know about me and Duc? Would you like to know my favorite color? Or perhaps my middle name? How about the size of my cock?" he says, in a caustic manner.

Tony whispers to Joe, "Jesus. This guy is a little rough around the edges, eh?"

"Yeah, unlike you, right?" Joe replied, sarcastically.

Sal laughs and shakes his head. "Sorry if I've done something to offend you, Dong, Duc. I mean no harm."

Duc replies to this one. "No harm? You, *foreigners*, come into our offices, flaunting that you control our nation's coffee economy, and threatening our autonomy."

"*Threatening*? Who's threatening you?" Sal said exacerbated.

Joe puts his hand on Sal's shoulder and cuts in. "If I may, gentleman. We don't mean to threaten anybody. Our intention is a partnership."

To this, Duc and Dong sit back in their chairs, seemingly interested. "Partnership…," remarked Dong.

"Yes, partnership. I'm sure you're aware of the growing popularity of supply restrictions within the coffee industry. Especially among the well-established countries."

Dong replies, "Yes, yes. Lots of other emerging markets are trying to take our market share."

Duc adds, "Prices have plummeted because of it. Lots of competition now."

"Yes! Yes! Exactly!" exclaimed Joe. "But what if there were supply restrictions? Vietnam, being the second largest exporter, would stand to benefit a great deal. You would be heroes to your constituents. What are your thoughts on proposing these restrictions at the next ICO meeting?"

Dong quickly replies, “Yes, yes. We’ve deliberated about this a great deal since the competition became fierce, but as you can imagine, the small countries would veto this proposal in a heartbeat. It would crush them. And any new legislation has to pass via a *general consensus*. It would just be us, Brazil, and maybe Colombia in favor. That’s nowhere near a general consensus.”

Sal starts talking again. “Well, we’ll never know if we don’t try. I say we make the proposal to the council and sell it as a win-win for all. Really harp on the fact that it’ll help price pressure on their countries' respective farmers. And then if they still have reservations, I think you’ll find Cosa Nostra has ways to bend the rules. But, of course, the fewer barriers the better. So getting the legislation passed would be ideal.”

Duc reiterates, “Bend the rules… As you can imagine, Mr. Conti, Dong and I are in highly visible positions of power. We don’t have the luxury you and your business partners have of ‘bending the rules'. There are consequences if we do such things. The public has transparency into our actions."

Sal nods and says, "We will take care of the dirty work. You two will be completely absolved of any 'rule bending' that is required." Sal points a thumb to Joe and Tony. "We have the best in the business here. These gentlemen have been in the game for years. They know how to take care of business efficiently, and discretely."

Duc and Dong look at Joe and Tony. The Vietnamese see the faces of two stone-cold, experienced, ruthless Sicilian mobsters. The very thought of what they have done in their past sends a shiver down Duc's spine. Their faces don't send a shiver down Dong's spine. He's seens plenty of ruthless killer, torturers, and other unspeakable types of people during his time at war. Although, he does notice a small ball of nerves bouncing around his stomach. That's a new feeling for Dong.

The two politicians take another long moment of silence to mull it over. Dong answers, "Well, as you can imagine, this will require a great deal of thought and discussion between me and Duc. Why don't you guys come back at the same time next week? I'm sure we will have an answer by then."

As he says this, he peers over to Duc, who nods in agreement.

"Of course," Sal says as he stands up to say goodbye. "We'll come back next week for an answer. Please feel free to give me a call in the meantime if you wanna talk through anything."

1

Eventually, the four men find themselves back in their respective hotel rooms. As Sal Conti closes his hotel room door behind him, his phone buzzes. It's Vinny.

"Hey, Vin! How's everything back home?"

"Good, good," says Vinny. "Not much other than the usual. Julia and I are in Como this weekend for a photoshoot she's doing. But I'm calling to hear about *you* guys. How's business going? We closin' deals? Buyin' coffee farms?"

Sal says, “Yeah, Vin! Things are happenin’ way faster than expected. We already closed deals on the first two farms on that list I made. Bought the first one outright and took fifty-one ownership in the other.”

Vinny exclaims ecstatically, “MY BOYS! You guys are *way* ahead of schedule! So we have a controlling interest in the two largest farms in Vietnam?!”

“Yeah, Vin,” Sal said smiling. “The family owns about forty percent of the country’s exports. Congratulations.”

“Congratulations to *you* guys!” Vinny says. “This is great news!”

“Yeah,” said Sal. “There is something you should know though, Vin. Not everything is going exactly according to plan. Tony got a little… emotional when were closin’ one of the deals.”

Vinny’s face darkens. “What do you mean, ‘emotional’?” he asked.

“Tony wasted one of the guys.”

"Oh for fucks sake. Why, what happened? Did anybody see it other than you and the boys?"

Sal says, "Well… the meeting wasn't going all that well. The owner seemed hesitant. Then, Tony felt like the bastard was making fun of the family, and that was the final straw. But not to worry, we got the situation cleaned up, the sale went through, and Gio and Nick are operating the farm as we speak."

Vinny says, "Your boys are really stepping up to the plate, eh? This is a difficult first job for anyone, especially two younger guys."

"Yeah," said Sal. "I'm really proud of them. The farm seems to be operating like usual, but I'll keep a close eye on it."

"Sounds good, Sal. Thanks for the update." Then quickly, Vinny follows up saying, "Glad to hear everything is going well, Julia finished up the shoot so I gotta go."

"Sounds good, talk to you later Vin–" but before Sal could finish, Vinny already hung up.

In the week between meetings with the ICO officials, Sal and Binh stayed in Hanoi so Binh could show him around. They went to bars and restaurants that are frequented by political officials, hoping to run into Duc and Dong or maybe other high–caliber individuals. Tony and Joe took a leisure trip to Thailand for four days. During that time, Joe had never seen someone eat, drink and fuck the way Tony did. He'd try to get Joe to "loosen up" for once by pulling him into these escapades. He even tried hooking Joe up with his One-Night-Stand's sister at one point. "We're brothers, their sisters. It's perfect!" he said. But Joe wouldn't entertain the idea. He is unquestionably loyal to his family. As a child of divorce, he couldn't imagine putting his kids through that. Plus, he deeply loved his sweet Josephine. Although, he did admire Tony's desire to live his best life — whatever that may be. On their last day in Bangkok Joe even mentioned how impressed he was that Tony had the wherewithal or desire to live in such a way, even if only for four days. Tony would reply to this by saying, "Yeah, well, you don't get any pleasure on the inside. So now that we are on a trip with the sole purpose being pleasure, I'm gonna take advantage. You never know how long your freedom will last."

That last comment bugged Joe. He never said anything to Tony about it, but it bugged him. It bugged him because if you do clean work, you won't need to guess how long your freedom will last. It'll be *perpetual* because clean work doesn't land you in jail. It made him feel like Tony knowingly does sloppy work because it's easy. He doesn't have a wife or kids to think about, so he takes shortcuts. This made Joe think, *But what about me? What about our father? Doesn't Tony want to stay out of jail for us? Doesn't he* care *about us? I mean shit, even if it was for Mom and Nicolette. Maybe he would have a halfway decent relationship with them if he wasn't too busy getting in trouble. Then again,* I've *never been arrested and I still don't have the best relationship with them.* Joe never said it, but the thought of not being close with his mother or sister, also hurt him.

3

Finally, a week zipped by, and before they knew it, the next meeting was here. They have the morning and most of the afternoon to kill, with the meeting being at five o'clock so Joe decides to go on a morning jog. He figured it'd be a great way to get to know the area a little better, and besides, after eating and drinking with Tony on their excursion to Thailand, he felt like he could stand to lose a few pounds.

At eight in the morning, Joe puts the finishing touches on his shoelaces and heads out of their hotel room. As he turns around to lock the door, something peculiar happens. A short Vietnamese woman, with most of her clothes still in hand, walks out of Sal and Binh's room. Joe stands there, dumbfounded, staring at the half-naked woman. As the woman sneaks out of the room, she glances quickly at Joe, smiles, and heads down the hallway to the exit.

The fuck? Joe thought to himself. *Sal and Binh havin' orgies in there?* He shakes this thought from his head and exits the building to start his run.

4

The hours pass, and it is time for the meeting. At four thirty Sal is waiting in the hotel lobby. Finally, Joe and Tony arrive.

"How are you boys doin'? Haven't gotten to talk to you much since your little… vacation," said Sal.

Tony answers, "Great. Those Thai women can bend in ways I didn't think were possible." Tony laughs at this, while Joe and Sal shake their heads in disapproval.

"Speaking of women," says Joe. "I saw the hooker walkin' out of your room this morning, Sal. The fuck are you and Binh doin' in there?"

Tony looks at Sal, smiling from ear to ear. He says, "Damn old man! Didn't know you had it in you. But with Binh? I mean he's a cute guy and all but–"

Sal cuts in and pointedly remarks, "Shut up, Tone. It's not like that. I uh, I got my own room. Binh wanted some company last night and I, of course, didn't want to be involved in any way, shape, or form."

"You got your own room?" asked Joe. "Sal, why are you friends with this guy? He kicked you out so he could call a prostitute! What makes you believe you can trust this guy? Why should *we* trust this guy? You know what? I don't think we should work with him anymore."

Sal quietly and quickly replies, "I trust him and you can too. He's been through a lot and has a few… rough coping mechanisms is all. Besides, I owe him one. We can't fire him."

Tony replies, "The fuck you mean you owe him one?" Right as Tony says this, the elevator dings and Binh walks out.

Sal quietly says, "Forget it." and greets Binh.

"Ready to close this deal?" asked Sal.

"Ready," replied Joe, glaring suspiciously at Sal.

5

The black Escalade pulls up to the familiar building where the ICO officials operate. Binh stays in the driver's seat, and the three Sicilians exit the vehicle and nervously walk into the building. As they enter the same lobby area, the receptionist sees them and quickly waves them to the desk. This time, nobody is waiting around.

She says nothing to them, but opens the door to Dong's office and waves them in. Sal walks in first and is greeted with that familiar wave of dung-smelling cigar smoke that hit him so heavily last week. “Gentlemen!” exclaimed Dong as he stands from his desk. Duc, who was sitting in the same chair the Sicilians saw last time, stands up to greet them as well.

Joe wonders to himself if Duc actually works in his office that is on the other side of the receptionist, or if he stays here in Dong’s office and spends all day serving as his Yes Man. *Probably the latter*, he thought.

The men all exchange pleasantries and take their seats. “So, have you had enough time to deliberate on our proposal?” asked Sal.

Dong replies, "Yes, yes. And we like it quite well. However, the deal feels slightly… shall we say, lopsided."

Sal gives a quizzical look to Dong. This pushback came as a surprise to Sal because he could sense the nervousness the two politicians encountered during their last meeting. He could feel it. He knew the Sicilians had instilled fear into the Vietnamese. What he didn't know, was that during the week between their meetings, Dong had a chat with Duc. The chat was meant to convince Duc that they needed to toughen up in the next meeting – instill fear into the Sicilians the way they had fear instilled in themselves. Although it seemed to Dong, that he was mostly trying to convince himself of this. He hated feeling like a puppet, and that's exactly how the Sicilians made him feel. Well, it was time for him and his partner to become the puppeteer.

Sal replied, "Well, as we said last time. You will have enormous power over any politician who threatens your seat. If this passes, you will be a hero to your constituents in the agriculture community.

The economy will be firing on all cylinders, and they will have *you* to thank."

"Yes," replied Duc. "But why should you be gaining money AND power, while we only gain power?"

"You want a slice of the pie?" asked Joe.

"Precisely," replied Dong.

Tony's fists tighten on his chair's armrests. Joe see's this, and gives Tony a "cool it" look. Tony's hands open up as he tries to relax.

Duc see's this as well and it makes him want to vomit. He hopes the closed fists will end up in Dong's face, and not his own.

"What did you have in mind?" asked Sal.

"We ask for a modest ten percent of your annual profit."

Joe quickly and hastily responds, "Ten percent of our profits?! These are already highly profitable farms *without* you intervening with the ICO. What makes you think your efforts are worth ten percent? *No way* you get ten percent."

Sal adds, "I'm afraid he's right, gentleman. We can't make ten percent work. Besides, you aren't contributing any expenses to the business. We are taking on one hundred percent of the risk."

"Well," said Dong. "The farms are in fact very profitable without us; however, without our intervention, your farms will not be *as* profitable as they could be." Dong takes a long drag from his cigar, and Duc follows suit.

Tony's eyes grow big as this happens. He's never seen someone be able to drag a cigar for that long without throwing up. This was not a normal human being.

"Tell you what," said Dong. "Five percent, and you have yourselves a deal."

The smoke-filled room grows silent. Joe and Tony sit back with their arms crossed.

Finally, Sal speaks up. "Two and a half percent."

Joe quickly sits upright. "Sal, what the fuck?!" he exclaims. "*No* percent. Not ten, not five, not even two and a half. None."

Dong and Duc look at Sal, ignoring Joe. "Do we have a deal, Mr. Conti?"

Sal takes a beat, and replies, "Yeah. You have a deal at two and a half."

Joe can't believe what is happening but stays silent.

Dong and Duc laugh happily, stand up and shake Sal's hand vehemently. "Wonderful, wonderful," remarked Dong.

Joe and Tony remain seated, refusing to shake anybody's hand. Dong and Duc look at Joe and Tony still seated, give each other a look of grief and internal worry, and sit back down.

Once they are all seated again, Dong says, "Let's talk shop then. The first meeting is in a month and a half. First week of September. Between now and then, there are plenty of political events and soirees I recommend you all attend. I will introduce you to those who will make all of our lives easier. People of power."

Sal says, "Good idea. It'll be good to make face and make sure the others know we are on their side."

Dong says, "Yes, yes. The last thing we need is for anyone in a position of power to make our lives harder because they think you foreigners are trying to exploit our hard-working people."

The room shares a moment of silence, mulling over what he had just said.

"Well," said Dong. "Anything else?"

"No," said Sal. "I think we're set then."

Dong replies, "Great! I will send you the list of events this coming month. Do you have a driver or translator available to all? We are happy to set you up with someone."

"Actually, we have one. Just haven't brought him around because he's a tad shy," said Sal.

Joe gives Sal a mysterious look. *Shy?* he thinks. *I think you mean chaotic, old man.*

Dong smiles. "Got it. Terrific. Well, Gentlemen needless to say, we are excited for the future."

“Likewise,” said Sal.

The three Sicilians get up, shake their hands, and exit the building, unsure about the challenges and dangers looming in their future. Although, they will soon be uncovered.

Chapter 6

Giovanni's Excursion

"Nick, you want to go to a bar tonight?" Giovanni Conti asked to his older brother.

Nick and Gio are currently working in the same structure where Nam Le's life abruptly ended. There is still a stain on the floor from Nam's blood and brain matter. The stain has been staring at Gio – haunting him. Nick is hunched over his own desks, trying to finish up paperwork to make payroll this week.

"A bar?" asked Nick. "What bar? And how are we getting there? We are *so* far away from Ho Chi Minh City. We can't just walk to a bar, get drunk, and walk home."

Gio says, "I already asked our translator, Liem. He said he'd drive us."

"I don't know how safe that is, Gio. We don't know the area at all," replied Nick.

"No it's okay! Liem said he'd stay with us and show us around. Take us to his favorite places even."

"Why do you want to go out anyway, Gio?" Nick asked.

Gio is silent for a moment. "I just feel like I need to take my mind off things here, Nick. I've been struggling as you know, and I think one night of just hanging out and getting away from this godforsaken hellhole of a farm would do me some good."

Nick sighs. "I don't think so, Gio. But I agree we should do something to get our minds off work. Maybe this weekend we can have Liem drive us to the city and we can get lunch or something during our break?"

Gio stands up and stretches his arms wide. He'd been sitting at his desk for so long he began to believe his muscles were *supposed* to feel like taught rubber bands. He then replies to Nick sulkily, "Yeah. That's fine. This weekend."

Gio slowly walks out of the structure to get some fresh air, as Nick keeps working without looking up.

1

Hours go by, and Nick finally exits the hut. *Thank god that shit is done*, he thought. Then, what he sees renders him breathless. He walks out into a stunning scene of the sun setting over the lush, green mountains. The soft sky is a cotton candy mix of blue, red, pink, and orange. The picturesque sunset makes him miss Sofia. The two of them would spend all evening at their favorite spot on a beach outside of Palermo, drinking red wine and watching the sunset. Sometimes Gio would tag along and make fun of how cute they were, in which case Nick would rip on Gio for not being able to pull any girls. Sofia found their brotherly bickering endearing. She used to say that's how she can tell they truly cared for each other. It would drive both Nick and Gio up the wall hearing her say that, but they both knew it was true. They cared deeply for one another.

After taking in the scenery for a few minutes, Nick walks toward their new home. When he enters, it is eerily quiet. No usual television noise blaring. "Gio?" he asked. Silence. *Must be on a ride around the farm with Liem or something*, he thought. He makes himself comfortable on the couch, and turns on the television. He and Gio signed into their Netflix account their first day on the farm, and figured out how to use a VPN to get shows from back home. Gio couldn't believe it. Good thing too, because having that little taste of home was arguably the only thing keeping him sane.

Five short minutes later, Nick is in a deep sleep on the couch.

2

Meanwhile, Gio is wide awake. He is breathing heavily, sweating, and surrounded by flashing lights. The noise is so loud his eardrums feel as though they might erupt. He and Liem are at his favorite club in Hanoi. The Hanoi Disco Club. People are stumbling all around Gio, spilling drinks on him, and themselves. This is the first club Gio has ever been to. He can't imagine why some people find this to be an enjoyable thing to do every night on the weekend. Especially since he's having a hard time enjoying this one experience.

Liem puts an arm around Gio. His breath reeks of beer. He slurs something in Vietnamese.

"WHAT?" shouted Gio, competing with the music. "REMEMBER, I DON'T SPEAK VIETNAMESE."

Liem shakes his head and says in Italian, "ARE YOU HAVING THE TIME OF YOUR LIFE, OR WHAT?"

"YEAH I'M HAVING A GOOD TIME," said Gio.

"WE NEED YOU TO HAVE THE *BEST* TIME, G. THAT'S WHY WE'RE HERE, RIGHT?" Liem then reaches for the bar they are standing next to, steals two shots of rice liquor off the table from people who are turned around, and hands one to Gio.

"BOTTOMS UP," he yells.

The two of them shoot the liquor, and it makes Gio's face squirm. But five seconds later, something happens. Gio gets a warm feeling in his stomach that he hasn't felt since drinking the Chianti at Vinny's house before they left for Vietnam. The warm feeling that only alcohol can provide. Like a hug, if a hug made you profusely vomit from doing it too much.

Gio loosens up a bit and yells, "LIEM, LET'S DO ANOTHER SHOT."

Liem smiles, gives him a thumbs up, and heads for the bar. Ten seconds later, he comes back holding four shots. Gio isn't quite sure how he has been getting the alcohol so fast with all the lines at the bar but doesn't question it. Instead, he cheers with Liem and shoots both shots back simultaneously.

Gio is really feeling good now. He hasn't even thought about the godforsaken farm in what feels like a lifetime. He is as loose as he's been since arriving in Ho Chi Minh City. A City in which he once felt dread. However, at this very moment, he is in love with the City. The lights, the music, the people, the liquor. He's in his element now.

After the shots, one beer goes down his gullet. Two. Then three. The night whirls on, the music gets louder, the lights shine brighter, and the people get more and more friendly. Gio now feels completely at ease. The drinks are smooth and his body is moving to the music. He can't remember the last time he felt this relaxed.

A few hours and who knows how many drinks later, Gio finds himself walking on a sidewalk outside. He is accompanied by Liem and three other people, stumbling and laughing together. The street is alive. Seemingly hundreds of people are out eating, dancing, and partying in the streets. It is electric. Before Gio can ask where they are going, they arrive at a food truck. The menu is blackboard of characters he's never seen before so he turns to Liem and says "Hey, order me whatever is good." Liem laughs, puts his arm around him, and gives him a noogie.

Five minutes later, Liem hands Gio what appears to be a slice of pizza. Gio takes it, confused.

What the– am I back in Sicily? he thinks.

Liem and the other three people start laughing uncontrollably.

Gio smiles, "I said that out loud, didn't I?" he said.

Liem, still laughing, nods and says, "Bánh tráng nướng. It's Vietnamese pizza. I figured the Italian boy would love it!" Liem said in Italian.

Gio smiles, takes a ginormous bite, and his eyes grow wide. Liem and the other three burst out in laughter again.

"Yes, yes! Good right?" said Liem.

Gio then finds himself in another club. He looks down at his hands because the last thing he remembered was that he was eating a Vietnamese pizza. The pizza is gone, but there is a slight sauce stain on his shirt. *Huh, must have eaten the food. How'd we get here*? he thought. He checks his watch, and it reads 12:00 am. *Or is that 1:00 am*? he wondered. *No, that says 2:00 am. Hmmmm... or* is *that 12:00 am*? Then Liem comes by with a beer and hands it to Gio. Gio shrugs off this thought and continues enjoying the lights, the music, and the beer.

3

Nick wakes up off the couch. He checks his watch, and it reads 2:00 am. He walks slowly and sleepily to the bathroom to expend his bladder. After he is done, he walks back to the bedroom where he and Gio sleep. Before crawling into his bed, he checks on the other bed in the corner to see if Gio is sleeping soundly or if he is having another nightmare. Except, Gio isn't there. *What the fuck?* Nick thought. "Gio?" he asked quietly, so as to not disturb his sleep in case he is in fact there. Silence. "GIO?!" Nick yelled. He begins pulling apart Gio's bed, hoping to find Gio buried underneath somewhere. But nothing.

He runs outside, and yells his brother's name again, only to hear it echo back to him. He continues running toward the shelter where their desks are and grabs the keys to the four-wheeler and a flashlight. Nick begins ringing Gio's cell phone, in hopes to get him, but it keeps going straight to voicemail. *His phone must be dead*, he thought. He starts the four-wheeler and zips off down the dirt road toward the thick farm of coffee cherry shrubs.

4

An hour later, Gio finds himself outside once again. Except, this time it is just him and Liem. The buzz and liveliness of the street is now gone. It feels empty. Desolate. Liem and Gio enter the Escalade they took to drive into the City.

"Are you sober? Can you drive?" Gio asked.

Liem doesn't respond. Instead, he shakes his head and makes a grunting noise as he reclines the driver's seat into a lying position. He then closes his eyes.

"Okay, we'll sleep it off, and get to the farm first thing tomorrow," he said.

Giovanni Conti lays down in the back row of seats and dozes off, feeling as though the car is floating in a river with rapids. He never liked rivers.

5

All the while, Nick is on the four-wheeler, driving around the dark thick maze of a farm. Two hours into his venture through the jungle, something catches his eye. *Is that what I think it is*? Nick wonders hesitantly to himself. He points his flashlight toward his gaze, and it illuminates exactly what he feared. It's a carcass picked clean. White bones, shiny with still-wet saliva cover the once-alive creature. He gags at the sight.

Nick thinks back to Binh's words when they first arrived. The thing about watching out for animals, but more specifically watching out for your sanity. That advice seemed to bother Gio a great deal.

Nick Conti is not a very religious man, but right then and there he prayed to God that his little brother's sanity isn't picked clean, buried somewhere in this god-forsaken jungle like the carcass. He then prayed that if that was the case, his sanity wouldn't be next.

Nick thought about giving up the search after seeing the carcass. It scared him a great deal. Not just because it meant animals were on the prowl and hungry, but because now he worried about his own psyche. Even then, he didn't give up. Not until he found his brother.

An hour after that, the sun finally came up. *Shit, I need to start the day. What the fuck and I gonna tell Dad?* he thought. *Hopefully he doesn't call until I find him.*

6

Giovanni wakes up three hours later, with vomit on his chest.

Ugh, he thought. *This better be mine.*

He sits upright quickly and almost falls back down. He feels like he is spinning. He musters up the courage to sit fully upright and check his surroundings. They are in fact, not floating on a river. *Thank god,* he thought. There is more vomit on the floorboard, and the seat next to him. He retches at the sight and smell of the foul piles of bile.

He climbs over the seat and sharks Liem awake. “Liem. Hey, Liem!” he shouts. Let’s go! We need to get back before Nick wakes up.”

Liem lazily opens his eyes, murmuring. He then gets out of the car and throws up on the street next to the car. “God. You don’t look good. Okay let me drive,” said Gio. He sticks his hand out for the keys.

Liem shakes his hand and replies, “You don’t know what a single sign here says. I’m good. I just need a second.” Liem stays staring at the ground and then vomits once more.

He wipes his mouth, smiles, and cheerfully says, “All right! Let’s get back to the farm!” then starts the car.

Gio cannot believe his exuberance right now. He wonders if this is how everyone who parties hard on the weekend acts after a night of drinking. *Are they just used to it?* he thought. There is no scenario in which Gio thought he could ever get used to this feeling. Nor does he ever want to get to that point.

7

They finally arrive back at the farm, and park the Escalade. Gio walks back to where he and Nick are staying, walks in and immediately takes a shower. *Hopefully Nick has no idea*, he thought. *This is good. If Nick wakes up, he'll probably assume I just woke up and started getting ready for the day.* When Gio gets out of the shower, he hears silence. He walks around the house and doesn't hear Nick. *Must still be asleep,* he thought. He enters their bedroom and sees his own bed is torn apart, and Nick's is nicely made. *Oh shit*, he thought.

He runs to the office where their desks are and sees Nick hunched over his desk. Nick quickly looks up at the sound of someone busting through the door and stands upright. He sees Gio standing in the doorway, looking like an absolute dumpster fire – as if he was in a street fight, had food thrown at him, and then threw up on himself.

Nick nailed that last assumption.

"Gio!" he yelled. "Are you okay?! What the hell happened? Where were you last night?"

Gio's face turns tomato red. He is too embarrassed to tell Nick that he went to a club, got so drunk he forgot most of what happened for the night and then ended it by throwing up on himself while sleeping in a car in downtown Ho Chi Minh City.

So instead he says, "I got lost."

Nick bursts out laughing. "Fucking lost?!" he said. "Look at you! You look like every American college kid in the movies who don't know how to handle their liquor. You ended up going to that bar, didn't you?"

Gio grins. Hearing Nick's laugh eases his embarrassment a little. "Yeah," he said. "Liem and I went to a few clubs."

"Well," Nick replied. "I'm glad you had fun, but this can't become a regular occurrence, Gio."

"I know. It won't become a routine, promise," Gio said looking at the ground. He suddenly looks up at Nick, eyes wide. "You have to promise you won't tell the others. Especially Dad or Vinny. If one of them finds out, I'll be deep underwater with the family. It'll ruin my reputation, Nick!"

Nick replies, "Yeah, yeah, Gio. I won't tell. If you let it happen again, I will. But this one stays between you and me."

Gio smiles. "Thanks, Nick. You're the best older brother a young mobster could ask for."

Nick smiles in return. "Thanks, Gio. You're not so bad yourself." He sits back down at his desk, to get back to work, but then looks back up at Gio. "Also, you gotta tell me about your night later today. I wanna hear how clubbin' went for a tall skinny Italian boy in Ho Chi Minh City. The ladies seem to like you for looking different than the rest of the bunch?"

"No action with the ladies," Gio replied. "I think most were scared off by the pizza stains on the shirt." Gio points to the red marks on his shirt.

Nick laughs. "Shit, I thought that was blood. Where the fuck did you find pizza in Vietnam?"

"I don't know. Liem just handed me a slice and said it's pizza," said Gio.

"Better than Sicilian pizza?" Nick asks pointedly.

Gio gives Nick a sardonic stare. "Nothing is better than Sicilian pizza, Nick. You should know that." Gio starts to walk out of the structure and says, "I gotta go lie down. I'll finish up the rest of my paperwork tonight."

"Sounds good, Capone,' replied Nick, smiling. "Go rest up."

Gio tips his fedora to Nick and heads toward their sleeping quarters.

Chapter 7

The Boogeyman

The date is Saturday, September 2nd. Location: Bogotá, Colombia. The first ICO meeting since the Sicilians purchased the Vietnamese coffee farms, is finally here. The meeting is strictly closed off to members only; however, that didn't stop Sal, Binh, Tony, and Joe from making the trip. They decided to travel to Bogotá with Dong Tran and Duc Pham. The hope was that they could meet with some of the officials from various countries. Tony mentioned it could be helpful to incite some fear in them as well if the vote doesn't go as planned.

Sal and Joe shut that idea down quickly.

The meeting room is a gorgeous mid-sized auditorium flaunting a smooth mahogany wood for the tables and chairs. There is a raised platform with one table facing the entry doors. The remainder of the tables face the raised platform as if to signify its importance. Sitting on the raised platform behind its long, mahogany table, is James Williams.

James is a tall, caucasian man with brown wavy hair and blue eyes. He is the only man who presides over the ICO council meetings. As a member of the English Parliament, many of the ICO members loathe the fact that James Williams presides over the meetings. The UK is merely an importing member, meaning they are solely buying coffee from exporting countries. Only about fourteen percent of ICO members are importing countries, meaning the vast majority of its members are exporting countries. The big exporters, namely Brazil, Vietnam, and

Colombia, believe it important to have an exporting member preside over the meetings since this person would have a better understanding of the needs of most of the ICO members.

The disdain for James is more symbolic in nature though, since the presiding member really doesn't do much aside from ensuring the conversation and voting occurs in a timely manner. Everything else is left to a vote and only passed via general consensus.

In the audience, there are two representatives per table from each member country. The last few representatives pile into the auditorium and find their seats. Duc and Dong are amongst the last. They pile into their table near the very back. They always hated that the tables are set up alphabetically by country.

There is a slight chatter amongst the members until a gavel wraps one of the mahogany tables.

Then silence.

"Thank you for your attendance," said James Williams. "It is with gratitude that I welcome you all to the final meeting of 2023. I would also like to extend a thank you to the Colombian representatives, and their country for being the gracious hosts of this meeting."

The audience lets out a gentle applause for this.

James continues, "Now, let's get started with the updates from each committee. We have a lot to get through today."

Each committee within the council presents an update on the state of the industry. Finance, Administration, Statistics. It's a long, laborious, process. So much so that Duc began to fall asleep. That is, until Dong elbowed him hard in the shoulder, jolting him awake. Dong looks around to check if James or any member countries saw this, but all are focused on the contents of the meeting. Good thing too, because the last thing they need is a bad rap from the other members before they propose radical legislation.

Finally, after two hours of news, updates, and statistics on the coffee industry, James Williams opens the floor for any ad hoc discussion or ideas that may be present.

Duc and Dong share and look. Then, Dong stands tall, raising his hand. James points to Dong, gesturing for him to speak his mind.

Dong says, “As many of you know, the exporting members of this council have come to face extreme price pressures. The country of Vietnam would like to propose that the ICO comes to an agreement to set supply restrictions on coffee exports.”

There is a slight chatter among the members.

Dong continues, “We are open to discussing exact terms on these restrictions, but we believe some action is necessary to keep our farmers and the industry from experiencing growing pricing pressure. How much longer can we expect our farmers to receive pennies per pound of raw coffee? Especially when those very beans are then roasted for ten minutes, and sold for four, five, even six US dollars or Euros per cup?! It’s classic exploitation!” Dong bangs his fist on the table and adds, “We need supply restrictions, and we need them now!”

The chatter amongst the members starts again and grows louder than it was before.

James Williams raps his gavel on the table again to get the crowd quiet so he can speak.

He says, “Very well. This will go to vote once we conclude on the details. How heavy of restrictions did you have in mind, Vietnam?”

Dong replies, “We propose a restriction to export thirty-five million, sixty-kilogram bags of raw coffee per year, worldwide.”

To this, there is an absolute rupture of chatter, gasps, and scoffs.

“Thirty-five million?!” James replied in a condescending manner, almost laughing. “You realize that is approximately *one-quarter* of the amount of coffee that was exported last year, yes?”

Dong smiles. “Why, of course, Mr. Williams. We are well attuned to the coffee industry as Vietnam is the second largest exporter in the world. You knew this, yes?”

James scolds Dong and remains silent.

Dong addresses the group again saying, "This is a win-win for everybody! Yes, it means our respective countries will be producing less coffee. But your country's farmers will have increased margins! They will be able to provide a better life for their families, for their children."

One of the Mexican representatives stands and vehemently says, "This is corrupt! This will *kill* all of the countries exporting less coffee than the big three. All of us who are trying to grow our country's coffee industry will suffer! Countries like ours, Peru, Rwanda, Burundi – all of us don't have the economies of scale you and Brazil have!" as he aggressively points to the Vietnam table and the Brazil table at opposite ends of the room.

The Mexico representative continues, "If we set export restrictions, the only countries who will be able to produce meaningful supplies of raw coffee will be Brazil, Vietnam, and probably Colombia. That's it. All of us," he says, gesturing to the greater crowd, "are out of business. Done."

There is more chatter and commotion in the audience.

More representatives get involved. Those representing the lesser exporting countries become increasingly heated. Brazil and Vietnam are trying to defend themselves, expressing why it is good for the farmers and their respective countries. Dong and Duc are not surprised to see Brazil immediately side with them and defend this proposal. The importing member countries sit there in silence, watching all this go down. Secretly, they would prefer the legislation not to pass. Not because they are aware that the Sicilian mafia is about to wreak havoc on the industry, but because then they will have to pay more for their coffee imports.

Finally, a representative from the United Kingdom (an importing member) stands tall and yells. "WE ARE IN FAVOR OF NO SUPPLY RESTRICTIONS! We feel it is our duty to stand up for the little man."

To this, the room goes wild. Both with cheers in favor, and jeers against. Duc stands tall and yells back, "That is because YOU get cheaper prices! You and the other importing countries are the reason for our increased price pressure!" Duc turns to address the greater audience. "Don't you see? *They* are the enemy!"

The auditorium erupts.

1

Tony, Joe and Sal are waiting outside the auditorium, hoping to eavesdrop in any way possible. Even though Binh made the journey with them to Colombia, they thought it best not to bring him to this all-important meeting. It didn't take much convincing on Joe's part before Sal agreed to this. Binh wouldn't come. With their ears pressed to the doors, the three men's eyes grow wide as they hear the auditorium erupt into chaos.

"Ya think those are cheers or jeers?" asked Tony.

"Both," said Sal.

"I think I hear more jeers than anything," added Joe. "I hope they know what they're doin' in there."

2

The arguing goes back and forth for two hours, albeit much more organized and productive than it began. James Williams grew tired of the belittling words between members and demanded order. He then led a detailed and productive discussion regarding the proposal.

3

During those two hours, the Sicilians waited outside the auditorium, unable to hear much more than an occasional applause. Although they usually couldn't tell what the applause was for. Once the second hour comes to fruition, Tony begins dozing off in the middle of the hallway. Joe and Sal are standing up, with their ears toward the door, when they both hear something that startles them.

It sounds like a chainsaw.

They turn to see what made them jump. It's Tony, snoring.

Joe takes his shoe off, and throws it at Tony, knocking him in the head.

“Ow! Joe! What the fuck! That’s the second time you’ve thrown a shoe at me since being here, where did you pick that bad habit up?”

“I don’t know. Something about your face that just makes me wanna do that,” he replied, and turned his attention back to the door.

Right when he turns back toward the auditorium, the door flies wide open, almost jarring his boat-sized nose.

Sal, standing beside him, snickers at this.

Joe scolds him.

After only ten representatives pile out, they see Duc and Dong.

The Vietnamese step to the side of the hallway with the Sicilians to talk.

“How’d we do in there?” asked Sal, abruptly.

“The vote didn’t pass,” replied Dong. “We got Brazil on board as we thought we would. Even got Colombia and India. But those assholes from Mexico, Peru, Rwanda… they convinced the rest of the countries to say no.”

Joe and Sal let out an exhausted sigh, in unison.

Tony, on the other hand, turns red in the face.

He sees two representatives walk out into the hallway wearing Mexican flag pins on their suit lapels.

He points to the gentlemen and yells, “These guys?! Are these the fuckers?!”

Dong and Duc turn their faces toward the ground, so the other members don’t notice they are associated with these strange men in the hallway, in any way.

Joe puts his hand on Tony’s shoulder, gently. “Tone. Relax,” he said.

But the soothing is useless. Tony rips Joe’s hand off his shoulder and comes bearing down on the Mexican officials.

He grabs one of them by the suit jacket, undoing the Mexican flag pin on his lapel, and shakes him.

“YOU THINK THAT WAS A SMART IDEA, BUDDY? OH-HO YOU’RE IN FOR A

WORLD OF HURT!" he exclaims, shaking the confused man.

Joe catches up to Tony, grabs him by both shoulders and rips him off the official.

The other representatives watching this, begin rushing down the hallway to escape the scene, worried a fight might break out. After just seconds, the hallway clears out, and it is just the Vietnamese, the Sicialians, and the two Mexican representatives, dumbfounded about what just occurred.

The official that Tony grabbed, slowly fixes his jacket, picks up his pin, and places it back on his lapel. The two of them slowly walk away. As they walk toward the exit, they continually look back to see who the man that just attacked them was. They can't figure it out. They have never seen him before.

What they don't realize is that these strange men in the hallway are about to collectively become their boogeyman. The clown hiding under their bed or in their closet. A fear they can't escape.

Just as the Vietnamese and Sicilians are about to exit the building, they hear the auditorium door open once again. Two men enter the hallway.

It's the Brazilian officials.

One of the men is tall, and burly, with dark skin and dark hair. The other seems to be a carbon copy of this first man, except shorter and more stout.

"Gentlemen," the tall one says. "It is a pleasure meeting you. My name is Gabriel Santos." Gabriel reaches his hand out to Tony, who is still red in the face.

The shorter one starts to speak. "And I'm Carlos Silva," he says, reaching out to shake their hands as well.

Gabriel looks at Dong and continues. "It's a shame your proposal didn't pass, Mr. Tran. I speak for all of Brazil when I say we have high conviction that supply restrictions would be a net benefit for the coffee economy."

"Yes, yes. Quite a shame." Dong replied, looking questioningly at Gabriel and Carlos.

The Sicilians, Vietnamese, and Brazilians all share a moment of silence.

Gabriel is the first to break the silence. “Well,” he said. “I’ll just cut right to the chase. Let’s set the restrictions you proposed.”

The Vietnamese and Sicilians look at each other, confused.

“What do you mean?” asked Dong. “We only had four countries on our side. We need a general consensus from the council to be able to implement any legislation in our respective countries.”

Gabriel smirks. “Says who?” he replied.

Another moment of silence.

Dong looks at Sal and says, “What do you guys think?”

Sal raises an eyebrow and replies, “Dong, remember when I told you Cosa Nostra has its ways to bend the rules? I meant what I said. I like where this conversation is going, and think it is more than doable on our end.”

Duc cuts in. “Just to be clear, you are talking about us implementing supply restrictions in

Vietnam, and you implementing supply restrictions in Brazil? Without the approval of the ICO?"

"Precisely!" said Gabriel. "We implement restrictions and allow the biggest farms in the region to monopolize our own countries' markets. Once the small farms go out of business, they'll have to sell their land for cheap. The big farms gobble up all the land, and reach a point of economies of scale we have never seen before. They become so cost-effective, they dominate the market in not only our own countries but globally as well. I mean, let's face it. Brazil and Vietnam grow more Robusta beans than any other country. We already have a cost advantage compared to Mexico, Rwanda, Peru, Burundi – all of those other nations! Their Arabica beans just aren't as cost-effective as Robusta." Gabriel steps in closer to the men he is speaking to and adds, "Now, imagine on top of that, we pile on the benefit of economies of scale! I mean, no country will be able to even touch us!"

"Well, what kind of restrictions did you have in mind?" asked Duc.

Gabriel smirks and replies, “Gentlemen. We restrict until the only farms we want around are left.”

To this, everyone laughs. There is a collective sensation of ease. The pieces are falling into place.

4

The next few months were a global blur in the coffee economy. The Vietnamese and Brazilian officials went rogue and got pieces of legislation passed in their respective countries to restrict coffee exports. It all happened so fast. Although, it had to happen fast because if they restricted their nation's supply for too long, other countries would gain market share as they became new exporting partners for important buyers like the UK, USA, or EU.

The restrictions were ruthless and covered more than just the supply. One Brazilian farmer even got arrested in his own country because the government found out he was in violation of selling raw coffee above the new price ceiling that was implemented. The law stated that farmers may not sell raw coffee for any more than $150 USD per sixty-kilogram bag. The average price at the time was $258 USD. This law made it so each bag of coffee may only be sold for a mere fifty-eight percent of what they normally sold for. It devastated farmers. In particular, the one that got arrested.

He got arrested because he was selling his coffee for $150 USD per bag. Now, many other farmers were selling at the price ceiling during those few devastating months, but this particular farm just wouldn't go away. The ICO officials were feeling threatened by the tenacity of this business, and the ability of it to stay open even under extreme pressures. Therefore, one day, without giving notice to the public, they changed the price ceiling to $149.99 USD for twenty-four hours. On that day, they arrested the poor farmer for breach of the price ceiling.

5

From early September after the ICO meeting to mid-November, Vietnam and Brazil consolidated the vast majority of their coffee industry, to merely three farms per country. A true Oligopoly.

While each of the two countries did incur a slight loss in market share due to exporting less quantity, the new legislation proved well worth it. As soon as the country's farms were operating under an Oligopoly, the supply restrictions and price ceilings magically disappeared. This meant Brazil and Vietnam were able to produce however much coffee they wanted, at whatever price. This outraged the farmers who went out of business.

Citizens were calling for the impeachment of their officials. Foul play, they called it. Many constituents even came close to being able to provide proof that the officials were, in some way, tied to the large farms that benefited from the price ceilings and supply restrictions.

> Although, as soon as someone would get close to proving this, they too, would disappear. Never to be seen again.

There was one Vietnamese lady who started getting far too close to proving the foul play. She did research on the farms. Even found out that one proprietor by the name of Nam Le had gone missing right after he sold the farm to an Italian company. *Italian company?* she thought. *I knew they liked to drink coffee, but why would they be interested in growing it? Especially here in Vietnam*?

She reached out many times for comment from Duc Pham and Dong Tran. Poking around to see if they had any information on the Italian company that bought Nam's farm, but they declined to comment every time. Finally, she got the ear of a local news reporter. She reached out to Duc and Dong one final time, saying she was going to take the evidence to a local newspaper, and gave them one more opportunity to comment.

They took action, but it wasn't in the form of a comment.

The morning she was going to the news station, she heard a knock on her door as she was eating breakfast. She went to see who it was but didn't recognize anyone through the peephole. When she opened her door, everything happened so fast. She saw three white men she didn't recognize. One had a nose so big she thought he must be the real-life

Pinocchio. The second was a short, older-looking man. And the third was a beefy, tall, man with short black hair.

Before she could greet them and ask who they were, she heard Big Nose say, “Do it, Tone.”

That was the last thing she ever heard.

6

Brazil and Vietnam started producing a gobsmacking amount of coffee, and at prices that were never seen before. The USA and other heavy importing countries were gobbling it up. Nobody could compete with the cheap coffee being produced by these countries.

By early December, farmers in various countries around the world began to feel the pain. They were dropping like flies.

7

These few months were incredibly hectic for Nick and Gio, who were running Nam Le’s pride and joy the entire time. The two boys had never been so busy in their young lives. They experienced what it was like to work fifteen-hour days, seven days a week. They arguably became the best coffee operators in the world. Something neither of them would ever have thought to be proud of.

Although in a way, it was a point of pride for each of them. This was their first assignment with the family, and boy, has it been a tough one. But the family knew that. They also knew the boys were kicking ass.

Of course, none of them knew about Gio's little excursion into Ho Chi Minh City that one fateful night when we threw up Vietnamese pizza all over his shirt. Nick never said anything to them because Gio had been solid ever since. No slip-ups. No mishaps. Just sheer focus.

They were firing on all cylinders.

Nick and Gio did have one incident they had to tell Sal and the other guys about, though.

It was a chilly evening, right at sunset on the farm the boys now called, *The Palermo Coffee Company*. The farm that used to be Nam Le's pride and joy – an important player in the Vietnamese agriculture economy – is now Sicilian-owned and operated. They thought it was a clever name. Definitely unique. Where else in Sicily can you find a coffee farm? Hell, where else in Europe?

Nick and Gio were finished with a long, long day of office work, and decided to drive around the farm and see how things were looking. As the boys walked out to the four-wheeler, they stopped to admire the incredible colors of the sky and clouds.

"No matter where you are in the world, the sky always flaunts its beauty, eh?" said Nick, gawking at the sky. He continues, "It don't matter if you're at the beach in Sicily, or in the thick of the jungle at the Palermo Coffee Company in Vietnam. It always flaunts."

The boys take off into the sunset, expecting an enjoyable ride and some time to wind down from an exhausting day. They did have an enjoyable ride, but they weren't quite able to wind down.

Not yet.

When they arrived back at the wooden structure they called an office building, they saw an unfamiliar car parked off to the side of the dirt road.

Gio and Nick exchange a look and slowly walk toward the seemingly empty, beat-up car.

As they peer in, they confirm it is empty – nobody is in it.

They exchange another look of confusion, and Nick asks Gio, "Think it's one of Liem's buddies?"

"No," replied Gio. "Liem told me he is going out to the city again tonight. I saw him leave before we went on our ride around the farm."

They remain silent, looking at the empty car, when suddenly a voice startles them both.

They heard "Xin chào!" which they both knew was Vietnamese for "Hello!" They have picked up on a few words here and there since being immersed in Vietnam. Although the learning has been exclusively from Liem and what they hear him say on the farm to the workers.

The boys jump and turn around quickly. They see a man and a woman walking towards them.

"Stop right there!" Nick yells in Italian and holds up a hand to gesture for them to stop.

The man and woman stop and look at each other, confused.

"They probably don't speak Italian, Nick. Try English."

"Shit, right," he said. "Do you speak English?" he yells from a distance.

"Ah, yes," said the man. "Well, I do anyway. She speaks Jawa – no English. I am a translator for her reporting."

"Reporting?" said Gio, shakily.

"Yes, we are independent reporters and heard of the news about a few Vietnamese and Brazilian coffee farms really taking off. We wanted to see what all the fuss was about and interview the geniuses behind the business," said the man.

"How did you hear about this news? You guys in the coffee business?" asked Nick.

The man smiles, but the woman has been stone-faced this entire time.

"No, Not quite. Her cousin, however," he said pointing the the woman standing beside him, "owned a coffee farm in Sumatra, Indonesia. He was unfortunately forced to close up shop recently and told us all about the new laws implemented in the two largest coffee-producing countries in the world. Called it a 'Coffee Cartel'. He then told us these laws are now reversed."

"And?" asked Nick. "You think I'm some fuckin' political figurehead or somethin'? Come to talk to us about the laws we made?"

"No, no," said the man. "We were hoping to simply visit with the farm proprietors. Get their take on the story. After all, there are always two sides to a story."

Nick and Gio remain silent, staring at the two strangers.

"Could you gentlemen point us in the direction of the proprietor of this farm?" he asked.

"You're looking at them," replied Nick, pointedly.

The man chuckles and translates this to the woman, speaking Jawa. The woman looks at him confused. Then turns to the boys, wide-eyed.

"Now," said the man. "What could two… I'm going to guess, *Italian* boys, be doing running the largest coffee farm in Vietnam?"

"We bought it," said Nick.

The four of them stand in silence.

"Very well," said the translator. "Mind if we ask a few questions?" he asked, taking out a pen and small notepad from his shirt pocket.

"I do mind," said Nick. "We are not in the business of answering to the Paparazzi. I suggest you both get out of here."

The man holds up a finger and says, "Well you know, we went inside that wooden structure earlier, hoping to find someone, but all we found were papers on a desk. Looks like an Italian Company bought the farm. Does that mean you guys are employees of this company? Or are you in fact the owners?"

Nick, feeling the pressure, slowly reaches into the back waist of his pants for his pistol as the man is speaking. Gio see's this, and his stomach turns to knots.

"I said no questions," replied Nick.

"Well, if you won't answer our questions, we are happy to speculate on the events that are taking place here," said the man smiling.

"No you won't," replied Nick.

He then instantaneously pulls the pistol out from the back of his waist and puts a bullet in the man's chest. The man goes down hard and fast, turning limp instantly. He then shoots toward the woman but misses. He tries again and misses a second time. His hands were shaking madly after realizing that man's life, was the first life he'd ever taken.

The woman runs towards him as he is missing his shots, and tackles him to the ground. She is screaming something in Jawa, and clawing at his face. Nick is struggling to get her off and feels a warm liquid run down from his nose into his mouth. He tastes blood. *Did this bitch break my nose*? he wondered.

Five long seconds drag on, as Nick is trying to get the Indonesian woman off of him when suddenly there is a loud cracking sound filling the air.

Immediately following the crack, Nick pushes her off. Her body is suddenly limp. Nick looks up, startled. He sees Gio standing behind him, with a smoking pistol in his right hand. He looks down and sees a bloody hole in the center of the woman's head.

Before Nick can say anything, Gio drops the pistol and vomits on the ground. That too, was the first life Giovanni Conti ever took. And he vowed to himself it would be the last.

Nick and Gio cleaned up the scene and spent all night burying the bodies and discussing what they should do with the car. They ended up driving it to a cliff on the farm the next morning and pushing it off. That is, after all, what Sal recommended they do. Now all they could do, was hope nobody came snooping for the reporter and her henchman.

Chapter 8

Sweet Nostalgia

December 11th, 2023. It is a mild-weathered day in Hanoi, Vietnam. Beautiful blue skies are stretched long, for as far as the eye can see.

Although instead of enjoying the blue skies and sunshine, Joe, Tony, and Sal find themselves back in a dark, smoke-filled office with Duc and Dong.

There is a letter on the desk. They are all silent, staring at the letter as Dong picks it up and reads it aloud to the room.

December 2nd, 2023

To the Vietnamese ICO Council

Representatives,

It has been brought to our attention, that Vietnam and Brazil have violated the International Coffee Organization's Code of Conduct, Article 5 Section 103. This article clearly states, no member country, under any circumstance, is permitted to propose or vote for legislation in their respective country, that contradicts the general consensus of the International Coffee Council meetings. *According to the secretarial records from our most recent meeting which took place Saturday, September 2nd, 2023, the general consensus of the council was to forbid supply and/or price restrictions on coffee exporting countries. As your country is in clear violation of this general consensus, we require you to reverse the laws that have been put in place, or we withhold the right to suspend your membership in the International Coffee Council, and the International Coffee Organization as a whole.*

Sincerely,
James Williams, Presiding Member of the International Coffee Council

Dong immediately comments, fuming, "Well, gentlemen, it's a damn good thing we reversed the laws we implemented already. The last thing Duc and I need is for our country to get kicked out of the ICO. Our constituents would vote us *right* out of the office."

Joe replies, "Well, like you said. We already reversed the laws. That letter is dated December 2nd. They sent that thing just a few days before we changed the laws back to normal. We're in the clear."

Tony adds, "Yeah. Plus, they would never be able to kick you or Brazil out. The whole coffee economy would just descend into anarchy, every other country would leave the council and set their own country's laws. It would be a free-for-all."

Dong pointedly replies, "Well, I think Duc and I have received enough heartache from the journalists and angry constituents who keep writing to us, and asking us for comments. You and your 'Family' better make all the work we just did, worthwhile."

Sal replies almost chuckling, "Dong, we already have! I mean, Brazil and Vietnam are the only meaningful coffee exporters in the world at this point, and we have substantial stakes in every single Vietnamese one. I mean, this is just the tip of the iceberg. The real cash flow begins now. Trust us, you'll receive a big payout. And a continuous one at that. Just keep your trust in us, that's all we ask."

Dong and Duc exchange an exhausted look, and each takes a long drag from their thick cigars.

"Very well," said Dong. "You are correct in that we are well-positioned. We are just under a great deal of stress trying to keep our reputations upheld in the highest fashion. But you men have time and again taken care of any… issues that have arisen. We greatly appreciate that support."

Sal says, "Of course. Anytime. We weren't kidding when we told you we know how to find ways around the rules."

The men in the smoky office exchange goodbyes, and the Sicilians exit the building. They are outside, looking for the Black Escalade that Binh drove them in.

Sal looks at his phone and says, "Ah, Binh texted me he may be just a few minutes late. He had to run an errand."

Joe says, "Of course he did."

Tony takes a cigarette out of a pack he had in his shirt pocket and lights it up. He offers one to Joe and Sal, who each decline. He shrugs and puts the pack back into his shirt pocket.

After a long drag, Tony says, "What do you guys think about taking a trip back home?"

Joe replies, "Good idea Tone. I was just thinking about that today. We're in a good spot now, strategically. I think we should. We can give Pops the rundown in person."

"I don't know about that, boys," said Sal. "I think you two should stay here. We don't wanna get cocky with our positioning quite yet. I can go back and give Vin the rundown though."

Joe laughs. "I don't think so, Sal. If you go back, so do we," he says pointing to himself and Tony.

Sal replies, "I'm the underboss. I'm the one who will report directly to Vinny. You two report to me. Don't be difficult, boys."

Joe smirks and says, "Well, you'll be *my* underboss once I'm the Don one day, Sal. When

Vinny steps down, you really think he's gonna choose you over his own son? I don't think so. Better get use to follow *my* demands, Sal."

"I've been loyal to your father for my entire life. I'm like a brother to him. He'll reward me when the time comes. Don't get cute with me, Joe."

"I guess time will tell, old man."

Sal, face turns red at this. "I'm eight years older than you, Joe. Don't belittle me with that 'old man' shit. I'll be the Don once Vin decides its time to step down. Me. Sal Conti."

Suddenly the black Escalade pulls up right in front of them. Tony stomps on his cigarette, sighs, and says, "Finally. Gettin' tired of you two bickerin'," and walks into the car.

Joe and Sal slowly follow Tony. "More like Sal *Cunty*," Joe murmured under his breath.

1

Back on the farm, Nick and Gio are taking a rest day from work. They really needed one after the craziness that was their past couple of months. Gio is laying on the couch, watching Netflix using the VPN that gets them shows from back home. He needed a little nostalgia today.

Nick is in the kitchen, grabbing a snack, when suddenly he gets a FaceTime call from Sofia. He immediately answers. “Hey babe!”

“Hi, baby! How are you and Gio doing on the farm?!” she says.

“Good. We got some crazy stories. I want to tell you about them in person though.”

Sofia gives Nick a disconcerting look. “I hope these aren’t bad stories.”

“Nah, no. Just some hectic things going on. We’re managing it well though. The rest of the family seem pretty happy about our work,” said Nick.

“Good!” Sofia replied. “You guys have been on that farm an awfully long time though. Wasn’t it only supposed to be one month?”

“Yeah. I’ll tell ya, we can’t wait to get off this fuckin’ farm. It’s been great showing the guys what we can do, but it’s gettin’ pretty lonely out here.” Nick smiles and adds, “I miss our dates on the beach.

They don't got no Tyrrhenian sea out here, you know?"

Sofia smiles softly and says, "Yeah baby, I know. I miss our dates too. But that is actually why I called! I wanted to talk to you about something."

"Let's hear it."

"Well," she started. "We just started Winter Vacation at University, and I was thinking I could take you up on the offer you mentioned before you guys left."

"What offer?" he said.

"The offer to come visit! I've never been to Vietnam, and I could use some inspiration for my book."

"Yeah, I don't know if they'll want you writing about what's going on out here, Sof."

"No, silly. Not about the family. About travel, and culture."

Nick says, "I think Gio can tell you all about Vietnamese culture, hah."

"What do you mean?" asked Sofia.

"Ah, nothing. Probably also another story best saved for in-person. But I love that idea, Sof! When could you get here?"

Gio looks up from the couch, confused.

"I'm looking at flights right now. I could get one that leaves tomorrow evening! It would get there the next day at noon. Does that work?"

Nick smiles from ear to ear. "Yeah!" he says. "That works great. Wow, I can't believe you were serious about coming out here!"

Gio mouths, *Sofia is coming out here?* to Nick.

Nick waves him off.

"Of course I was serious! Okay, well I'll book this flight now! Wait. How do I get to the farm from the airport?" she asked.

"Oh, we have a translator and driver for us on the farm. We'll send him to get you, and I'll go with," Nick replied.

"Yay! Is it so romantic there?" she asked.

"Hah. It's… uh… no. Not romantic in any way imaginable."

They both share a laugh.

“Anywhere with you is romantic, baby,” Sofia replied.

Nick smiles. “You too, Sof. Well send me your flight info once you have it and I’ll make sure me and Gio are there to get you!”

“Sounds good!” she said. “I’ll send you the info in a sec. See you in no time, baby!”

“See you soon, babe,” he replied.

Once Nick hangs up, Gio says, “Sofia is coming?! Man, she must really love you to come to visit this hell hole.”

Nick laughs. “Yeah, I’m one lucky guy, eh?”

Gio gets off the couch, grabs a glass, and begins filling it with water from the faucet.

“I better not hear your headboard bangin’ in the middle of the night, Nick. We share a bedroom!”

“Relax, Gio,” Nick replied. “We’re quiet lovers. You won’t hear a peep.”

“YUCK!,” Gio said. “You better be kidding.”

Nick chuckles. “Yeah, Gio. I’m kiddin’.”

On that same day, Joe, Tony, and Sal are in first class on a Boeing 777 heading to Catania. Sal is still quite heated that Joe and Tony ignored Sal's request, nay, *demand*, for them to stay in Hanoi. He is growing paranoid that something terrible will happen while they are away. That they will lose the great progress they've made in Vietnam. He can't explain why, but he's usually right about these kinds of things.

Joe is sitting next to Tony, writing something on a notepad.

"What you writin' there, Joe?" Tony asked.

Without stopping or looking up, Joe replies, "Making a quick list of items I wanna run by Vin. Some notes. Tryin' to get my thoughts sorted out to give him a quick, clean, story."

Tony looks over at his writing and sees, in all caps, *TELL HIM ABOUT SAL'S DUMBASS JUDGEMENT.*

Tony snickers, shakes his head and turns back to the movie on the screen in front of him. He is watching the first Godfather, thinking about how if he were in the movie, he'd be the hardest one of the bunch. Hands down.

Many, many hours later they touch down in Sicily. Joe and Tony head directly to Joe's house to see Josephine and the girls, while Sal goes home to unpack and unwind.

As Tony and Joe walk to the front door of Joe's house, Tony says, "Joe, you have no idea how excited I am to see my little nieces. I didn't get to see them before we left! It's been even *before* I got locked up."

"Yeah, well, maybe you shouldn't have gone to jail. Coulda seen them plenty, then." Joe replied, giving Tony a stern look.

"I know, I know. I fucked up. But hey, I'm excited now, don't ruin this for me."

Joe smiles, pats Tony on the back, and says, "They've been telling me how excited they are to see Uncle Tony. That's all I heard when I told them we're coming to visit."

Tony grins as wide as he has in the past five years.

They get to the front door, and Joe knocks.

Julia DiGrasso answers the door. Joe and Tony stand there, confused. *What the– did we go to Pa's house?* Tony thinks. Joe has the same thought.

"Hey boys!" she says.

"Ayyyy!" they hear a crowd behind her say.

They smile wide. "Hey, Jules." The guys walk in, and their smiles grow wider. "Hey everybody!" they say in unison.

In the house are Julia, Vinny, Josephine, and Joe's girls, Sara and Anna. There is a wonderfully nostalgic smell of pizza dough and red sauce. Joe's mouth begins watering. Josephine makes the best pizza dough and red sauce. They didn't realize how much they missed home until just now.

Sara and Anna run quickly to their Father and Uncle. Sara tackle-hugs Joe, and Anna tackle-hugs Tony. Then they switch. The guys can't remember the last time they've felt this much joy. The last time they'd smiled this much.

Vinny walks over to them singing The Boys Are Back In Town by Thin Lizzy and hugs them both simultaneously. "Man! Those Americans have some good music, eh?!" he said. "They have a song that perfectly captures ANY moment!"

"They don't got no Sinatra over there, but they got some good stuff," Tony replied.

Josephine walks over to Joe after everyone has said their hello's, and plants a long, soft kiss on Joe's lips. "Welcome home," she said, smiling wide.

"Thank you. Good to be back," Joe replied. His face is now hurting from smiling.

"That pizza I smell, Jo?!" asked Tony.

"Why, yes it is! The family-favorite recipe, too."

"Oooooh boy!" said Tony, running into the kitchen to see the beautiful pizza pie.

Josephine turns to Joe and says, "We have about an hour until the dough is completely thawed. I was thinking we could play a little tennis out back?"

Joe replied, "Yeah! Let's play doubles with the girls though, I'm gonna need all the help I can get. Did you know there is not a single tennis court on *any* of the coffee farms we bought?"

Josephine laughs. “ Notta one?! That’s fine. I’ll even give you Sara since she’s older. Hope you’re not too rusty, baby. I had a lot of time to practice while you were away.”

“Haha, I’ll bet you did! Just gotta get changed,” Joe said. “One sec!” then he runs upstairs to change in their bedroom.

The rest of the people in the house walk outside to the backyard. The back has about 3 acres of green grass. There is a green-top, concrete tennis court, in the dead center of the yard. The way the sun hits it in the afternoon, makes it appear like a theatrical stage – the light beams all focused on Josephine’s sanctuary.

Julia says, “Wow, this is absolutely gorgeous! Vin, why don’t we come here more often?”

“We should!” he said. “As long as Josephine here doesn’t humiliate me in a match every time we come over,” Vinny said, winking at Josephine.

Joe and Tony come walking out of the house simultaneously. “Ready to lose, Jo?!” he exclaimed.

Josephine laughed, and let him have that one. "Sure!" she said.

As Josephine obliterates her husband in a match, Tony, Vinny, and Julia walk to the shade, and sit on the patio furniture under a large, bellowing umbrella. Tony and Vinny get to talking.

Vinny turns to Tony and says, "Tone. How's everything?"

Tony looks and him, questioningly.

"I heard that was a slight mishap at the first farm. But everything was taken care of, *cleanly*, yes?"

"Yeah for sure, Pops. The asshole farmer was making a mockery out of the family so I wasted him. I know it wasn't the most thought-out move, but I made it right. We got the farm, we cleaned up the situation, and anyone who comes digging around with questions about it has been… handled, as well," he responded.

"Good, good. I've always loved your passion. The way you protect what you love – who you love.

Just make sure we're making the smart decisions as well, eh?"

"Yeah, Pops. I'm tryin'."

Vinny nods. "How are Joe and Sal gettin' along?" he asked.

"Oh, man. They started off okay, but it's been turning into a bicker-fest lately."

Vinny raises an eyebrow at this.

Tony sees this and responds, "It's status this, status that. They're too similar so they bicker. That's why me and Joe are like two peas. We're so different, we don't bicker. What do they say, opposites attract?"

Vinny laughs. "I don't know about 'two peas', son. You guys have your fair share of arguments."

"Yeah, but this is different, Pops."

Vinny nods, lets these words soak in, and a silence falls among the three of them, as they watch Joe and Sara get torn apart in a tennis match against Josephine and Anna. Sara has been returning well, but the opposing side keeps hitting the ball toward

Joe, whom they believe to be the weak spot. They appear to be correct about that.

Tony turns to face Vinny again. “There’s somethin’ else I gotta tell you, Pops.”

“You sound serious,” he replied.

Tony starts, nervously, “It’s just that… Joe has a right to be bickerin’ with Sal on some of this stuff.”

Vinny looks questioningly at Tony. “What do you mean, son? Something that’s been bothering you as well?”

“Well, it’s a matter of trust. You know how we hired a translator that Joe was hesitant about? Turns out, Joe had a right to be hesitant. The translator, Binh is his name, is a bit of a hot mess.”

“What do you mean, ‘hot mess’?”

“Drinking problem,” said Tony. “We’ve caught him drinking on the job a few times. He’s also a little erratic. He hired a prostitute one night and made Sal find another room in the middle of the night.”

Vinny looks very surprised at this.

Tony continues, "Sal said somethin' about owing him? I don't really know. As soon as we started pressin' him about it, the fuckin' guy came into the room. We haven't discussed it since. I'm just worried we can't trust the guy. He seems… chaotic. And yes, I know, I know, you guys think I can be chaotic at times, but at least I don't have a drinkin' problem, ya know?"

"Wow…" said Vinny. "I mean, I usually feel like we can trust Sal's judgment. But that comment – the one about Sal owing this guy something… that concerns me. And you were unable to determine why Sal owes him?"

"Yeah. No idea," said Tony.

"Awwww come on!" yelled Sara, as a ball hit her father in the chest. "Dad, do you even remember how to play tennis?"

"Yeah, yeah. Your mother has a strong serve is all. You know, your Dad was a star athlete back in the day, Sara. It's just been a while is all," he replied.

Snarkily, Sara turns away and says, "Seems like it's been a *long* while."

3

Meanwhile, Sal walks into the front door of his house in Palermo. It is a modest house, far different from anything the DiGrasso's live in. No gold, no white marble countertops. Just a mid-sized, middle-class-looking house.

It's not that Sal doesn't make good money with the Family. In fact, he is on par with what Joe and Tony make, although he is unaware that it is slightly under their salaries. No, he lives modestly because when his wife Teresa became ill, they were told how much the medical bills might cost. Even before she became ill, they lived fairly modestly. They liked to spend their money on travel more than anything else, so they were perfectly happy living in a middle-class house if it meant they got high-class travel.

As he walked into the house, he noticed something peculiar.

Silence.

He hasn't heard silence in god knows how long. He's either been living in a small room with

Binh, dealing with Tony's bullshit, or arguing with Joe. He did have one night in his own room – the night when Binh hired a prostitute and Sal had to leave. Although, he could hear all the downtown Hanoi ruckus from that hotel room. Therefore, he didn't count that as silent, alone time.

It's a wildly comforting feeling, to be in silence. He can spend his time however he chooses. How often does he get to choose what to do for fun?

He decides the fun for the night will be reading the paper. Not the American paper that inspired the Sicilians to buy the coffee farms in Vietnam. No. A Sicilian newspaper. He needs a little taste of home. An hour goes by, and he gets tired of reading. That relaxing feeling of being alone begins to turn into loneliness. His boys are halfway around the world, his wife is in heaven, and he is the only one who remains in a once-filled, middle-class home in Palermo, Sicily.

He sits on the couch, and he turns the television to channel seven, Teresa's favorite news station. He doesn't really watch, though. The sound of the familiar news anchor voices takes him back to when Teresa was still alive. Back when she and Sal were in their early thirties and Nick and Gio were just young kids, running around the house causing a scene, as kids do. Those were the best of days. The days that taught Sal how to love. To love as a husband and as a father. He didn't realize at the time how lucky he was to have all those he loved under one roof. Life is like that sometimes – it moves so quickly you don't realize you're the luckiest bastard on earth, until you're not-so-lucky anymore.

Now, he realizes how lucky he was back then. He can't help but wonder what his boys are doing right now.

Nick and Gio just hung up the phone after speaking with Sofia. Gio says, "We should call Dad. Make sure he got back okay."

"Yeah, good idea," Nick said.

Nick goes to his Dad's contact in his phone and clicks on the FaceTime button. Gio rushes to stand side-by-side with Nick, so he is also in the camera.

Sal feels his phone buzzing, and it takes him out of his daydream. *I'll be damned,* he thought. *Their ears must've been ringing.* He goes to answer the phone but then pauses. *Is it ears ringing when someone is thinking about you, or just talking about you?* He shakes his head, realizing it doesn't matter, and answers the phone.

"My Sons!" he exclaims.

"Hey Dad!" they said in unison.

"How are things at the farm?"

Gio replies, "Oh you know. Living the dream at the Palermo Coffee Company."

Sal laughs. "The what?"

"The Palermo Coffee Company. Just a silly name we came up with for the farm," said Nick. "How's home? We wish we could be there with you."

"I wish you guys were here too. I was just thinking how it's a little too quiet around here with you guys on the other side of the world, and your mother gone and all…" Sal trails off, seemingly in deep thought about something. "But yeah, good! Good," he said, coming back down to earth.

Nick and Gio frown, and look at each other. They were both worried about their father going back home alone, but they assumed he'd be with Vinny most of the time.

"Got any plans while you're back? You're doing Christmas with Vinny and the guys, right?" Nick asked.

"Yeah, yeah. I'm seeing Vin and the guys for Christmas. Vinny is having all of us over for the holiday. I'm really looking forward to all the wine and food he is gonna have. He hosts his immediate family every year so he has the formula for a successful party."

"Sounds great, Dad," said Nick.

"What about you guys? I'm really sorry we couldn't have you two back here for the holiday…"

"No worries, Dad!" said Gio.

"Yeah, no worries at all. Gio and I are gonna have a ball. We found a food truck that serves

Vietnamese pizza, so we're gonna get a few of those for dinner. Have a little taste of home."

"Vietnamese pizza?! Where did you two find somethin' like that?" Sal questioned.

Nick peers over at Gio with a grin on his face, thinking about Gio's wild night-out. Then he says, "Our translator, Liem actually showed us. Said he thought it'd make us feel at home."

"Good!" said Sal. "Glad you guys are experiencing new things while you're there."

Gio nudges Nick over so he can be centered on the screen. "Yeah, it's been great trying new things, Dad. We do miss home though. Have you been able to get any word on when we'll have someone else to take over operations full-time around here?"

"Yeah, I assumed this conversation was coming soon. Sorry boys we haven't come all that close to getting someone quite yet. Just been so hectic getting everything else squared away. After the holiday, we'll prioritize it. Promise."

Gio half-heartedly smiles and says, “Okay. Thanks, Dad.” He was really hoping they would have found someone already and they would magically get to go home for the holiday. Alas, that was not the case, which disappointed Gio. Even though he knew this wish was far-fetched, there was a part of him that believed his father would do everything in his power to ensure his boys were home for Christmas.

“Well, say hey to the guys for us,” said Nick.

“Will do. Thanks for calling.”

“Of course,” he replied. “Bye, Dad.”

“Bye, boys.”

Nick hangs up and turns to Gio, who is visibly upset. On the verge of crying, even. Nick hasn’t seen him like this in a long, long time.”

“What's wrong, Gio?” he asked both genuinely concerned and also a little annoyed that he might have to console his baby brother.

“I just thought Dad would have found someone to take over by now and we’d get to go back home for Christmas is all.”

"Aw come on, Gio. It's not so bad. Sofia is coming up tomorrow! Us three will have a great time."

Gio smiles, this time more genuinely, and says, "Yeah. At least we'll be with *some* family!"

"Yeah! Exactly. We'll have the best Christmas yet," said Nick. Although, both of them knew that was a lie. The best Christmas they have had, and will ever have, was the last Christmas they had before their mother passed away.

Nothing will beat that memory.

Chapter 9

The Witches' Cauldron

Four days before Christmas, Sofia finds herself in the clouds, flying high somewhere over the South China Sea. She is about to arrive in a foreign country for the first time in her life. Her stomach churns and bubbles, like a witches' cauldron of emotion. Nervousness, excitement, anxiety, inspiration, adventure, doubt – it's all there, just brewing inside of her.

Although once she finally lands, and sees Nick Conti's face for the first time in six months, all of that fades away. She suddenly only feels one emotion: love. Sofia drops her bags on the ground at the Ho Chi Minh City airport and runs faster than she ever has in her young life toward Nick. Once she reaches him, she covers his face with kisses.

Gio, happy for them but disgusted at the same time, walks over to the bags she dropped to carry them to the car.

Sofia sees this and says, "Gio! You gentleman! Thank you for grabbing my bags. Come here, I've missed you so much!" She walks over to him with her arms out wide and bear hugs Gio, who tries to hug back but can't lift his arms very high because of the heavy bags in his hands.

"Missed you too, Sofia," he replied. "Nick and I have been pretty lonely on the farm, we're excited to have some time with someone else."

Liem drives the three of them back to the farm, where they will all be sharing a small room with two small beds. Not the nicest accommodations for Sofia's final Winter Break from school, but it doesn't matter to her as long as she is with Nick.

When she sees the digs for the first time, she lets out an audible laugh. *How the hell have these two lived in such tight quarts for* six months*?* she wondered.

"What are you laughin' at?" said Nick, also laughing. "I told you the family hooked us up with a sweet setup. Was I wrong?" gesturing toward the rinky-dink kitchen and living room as if it was a grandeur masterpiece of architecture.

Sofia laughs even harder at that. "Yeah, this penthouse is the hottest place to be for young college girls on break like me." She walks into the bedroom and asks, "So, one bedroom and two beds, huh?"

"Yeah," said Nick. "We're bunkin' with Gio. Hope that's okay. He can sleep on the couch if need be." Nick shoots Gio a smirk when he says this.

"If you two start gettin' frisky in the middle of the night, I definitely will be on the couch."

"Well, I think we can arrange for that to happen," said Sofia, grinning at Nick.

Gio groans and heads to the front door. "Wanna go for a ride around The Palermo Coffee Company? We'll give you the full tour."

"Yes, definitely!" she replied, genuinely ecstatic to see the land. Nick has told her how beautiful the sunsets can be here, and she is looking forward to sharing some romantic moments with Nick, the way they used to share on the Palermo beaches in the evenings.

Nick and Sofia take one four-wheeler, and Gio takes the other. The three of them ride off into the afternoon, zipping in and out of coffee bushes with their vehicles.

After a couple of hours of fun, they get hungry. "Let's get some food. Whaddya guys say?" asked Sofia.

"Ah," said Nick. "I can make you something back at the bachelor pad. We don't have much but I can do…scrambled eggs, a-la-mode?"

Sofia is taken aback. "Ew, what the fuck? A-la-mode, as in scoop-of-ice-cream-on-top, a-la-mode?"

Gio cackles at this. He forgot how abnormal they've been living the past six months.

Nick shrugs, chuckles, and says, "yeah we should probably go to the store, eh?"

"No, no. Let's go into the City! I wanna immerse myself in the culture while I'm here. Experience what it is like to *live* here!"

Nick will do damn near anything to make Sofia happy. So for the first time since Nick has been in Vietnam, he goes into Ho Chi Minh City, with the intention of having fun.

The three of them ate street food, went to a bar, and even went dancing. That's saying a lot because Nicholas Conti does not dance. He has a strict rule about not looking like an idiot (which he does when he dances); however, he can't say no to Sofia.

They ended up having such a good time, they did the same thing every day until Christmas. The three of them couldn't believe how much fun they were having in Vietnam. Then again, isn't having fun more about who you are with, rather than what you are doing?

On Christmas day, they decided to change up their activities for the day. The three of them decided on staying in – watching *The Godfather*, and exchanging gifts. They all wanted a nice, quiet day spent together.

While they were all squished on the couch together, watching the movie, Gio asked, “Are your parents upset that you're not with them for the holiday?”

“Yeah,” replied Sofia. “But tough. They’ll have to deal with the fact that I just had to see my man for Christmas this year.” Sofia smiles at Nick as she says this, and Nick returns a smile.

“Wow, I’m so grateful you chose me over them,” replied Gio.

“Not you, dumbass,” said Nick, smiling and playfully punching Gio in the arm.

“Well, him too!” said Sofia. “You both are my boys! I wouldn’t want the holiday to go any other way.” With that said, they turn back to the film and enjoy a jarringly realistic depiction of their lives on the screen.

1

Meanwhile, in Palermo, the DiGrasso family and Sal are enjoying the day together. Possibly the only time all of them have truly enjoyed a day together. Josephine's one wish for the holiday was that everyone got along. Not business talk, no fighting, no one-upping each other. There was business talk, but she at least got her other wishes.

Joe spent a few hours getting his ass kicked by each of his daughters at Tennis. Josephine didn't even give him a chance. She figured it wouldn't be the best for Sal to see him lose so badly to his wife. The guys in the family – and really all of Sicily – are a very proud people. Probably *too* proud. In her opinion, they spent way too much time worrying about looking tough – manly. Their reputation was everything; therefore, she spared her husband. Although he lost pretty badly to his seven and ten-year-old daughter. She wasn't sure if that was a much better look. Then again, old Sal Conti would have lost by an even greater margin to both of the daughters. She figured he knew it, too. That's why he didn't accept the challenge from either of them.

Tony, Vinny, Julia, and Sal played Bocce ball while Joe was busy getting swept by his daughters. Josephine was standing outside the court, yelling instructions at whichever daughter was playing against Joe at the time. At one point in a match with Sara, Joe yelled, "Hey Jo! How about some advice for your husband, eh?"

"Yeah, it seems like you need it. Okay, how about… don't suck?" she said snarkily.

"Ha-ha, " he replied sarcastically. "Great advice, babe."

Once they all got tired, they went inside to drink some wine, and watch old Italian Christmas movies. Meanwhile, Josephine was in the kitchen putting the finishing touches on the biggest, and most saliva-inducing feast she has ever prepared in her life. Even she couldn't believe how well everything was turning out. This was shaping up to be the best Christmas yet.

Once it was ready, they feasted. When they cleared their plates, they feasted a second time. Then a third. By the end of the night, everyone was so full they could hardly move. They couldn't eat a single bite of anything else. That is, of course, until the affogato came out. They ate the ice cream and coffee combination faster than they ate their dinner.

Once dinner was complete, and everyone filled up their wine glass, they continued the old Italian Christmas movies. Just one hour in, damn near everyone in the room was asleep or in between consciousness. The only one fully awake was Josephine, who couldn't sleep because she was soaking up every minute of her husband and kids all being under one roof again. Moments like these should never be taken for granted. Fortunately, she realized her luck before it was too late, unlike Sal Conti.

It was a good thing they were catching up on their sleep because if the Sicilians had any glimmer of what was going on Christmas day, 2023 at the Port of Veracruz, Mexico sleep would be the last thing on their minds.

2

While they were filling up on red wine and affogato, the Mexico, Peru, Rwanda, Burundi, and Uganda ICO representatives were together at the Port of Veracruz in Veracruz, Mexico, mischievously scheming. The Mexican official walks over to the individual operating the shipping container crane. "All of this," he says as he points to a group of shipping containers, stacked up three tall, and ten containers wide.

The crane begins lifting each individual container and placing it on a barge in the Gulf of Mexico. Each container is filled with raw coffee from all the countries present at the port today. Yes, Rwanda, Burundi, and Uganda have ports closer to them. Even Peru. But this was part of the deal.

You see, while the Sicilians were away, the Mexican representatives reached out to the other various high-growth countries with a proposal. The proposal was to go rogue from the ICO and create an

Oligopoly themselves. They all met in Veracruz to discuss the details.

"We partner with specific importing companies to buy raw coffee from our respective countries, exclusively. The benefit of doing so is ten percent off the entire coffee order. But they have to purchase *exclusively* from us," said the Mexico representative, when explaining the proposal.

"Even at ten percent off, we can't compete with Vietnam and Brazil from a price perspective. Why would they agree to this deal?" asked the Peru representative.

"Because," Mexico replied. "Are you familiar with the type of bean that is grown in Brazil and Vietnam?"

The people in the room look at each other, silent.

"Robusta beans!" he exclaimed. "We are all proud producers of the best Arabica beans the world has seen. All the importers know that Arabica beans are far superior in quality to Robusta. At ten percent off our current prices, this is a great deal for the buyers to get a high-quality bean, at an affordable price. The only stipulation is that they have to buy from our countries, and our countries only. But that still gives the buyer a terrific variety."

The other countries agreed to this proposal, and two weeks later, they were in Veracruz again, seeing it come to life. It wasn't all smooth sailing though. The reason they were at the port in Veracruz is because only one importer found their proposal worthwhile. And that importer only purchased coffee from the port of Veracruz.

This particular buyer, Mattingly & Son, Inc., was desperate for business. They were a coffee wholesaler who just opened up shop that very year, and were open to any deals they could get their paws on. Although, the ICO officials weren't aware of their desperation. Mattingly & Sons, Inc. caught wind that other importing companies were passing up this deal proposed by these countries and saw an opportunity. The opportunity – become the supplier of the most premier, exotic coffee around the world. Of course, they couldn't compete with the prices of already large importing companies, so their strategy was to provide the best *quality* products from around the world, so they could charge higher prices. And they would start with the coffee industry.

The cheapest port for Mattingly & Sons to buy from was Veracruz. The Mattingly family had connections to politicians in Veracruz, who were providing subsidies to the company if they bought products from the port. The politicians were hoping to spark the economy in Mexico and the surrounding countries that ship out of Veracruz. Their hope was to make the port as vibrant as Port Santos in Brazil. Of course, the infrastructure wasn't quite there for Veracruz to be as big, but that was the promise they made to their constituents.

Since the Mattingly family knew Mexico, Burundi, Peru, Uganda, and Rwanda were having no luck in their proposals, they knew they had the upper hand. The Mattingly family said they would be their only customer, under the stipulation that they only bought out of Veracruz.

The fact that Mattingly & Sons, Inc. had the power to only buy beans from one port was causing the African countries quite a bit of cash. They would need to have the coffee shipped to Veracruz, just to appease one buyer. But if it meant taking market share away from Brazil and Vietnam, it was well worth it.

Because of the discount, this one buyer purchased three times the amount of coffee they typically do. And they purchased coffee from every country involved in this new deal. A true win for the growing countries, albeit a small one. They were playing the long game. Take market share from the big guys, reach economies of scale, and be able to produce even cheaper coffee. If they could do this, a ten percent discount would soon undercut the market price of Brazil and Vietnam's raw coffee exports.

As the crane operator is moving shipping containers onto the barge, the Mexican representative noticed something. “Hey! Hey!” he yelled and ran to the operator waving his hands high in the air.

The operator stopped and looked at the guy, questioningly.

He points to a shipping container. "That container is not in our order. That is a mistake," he said. The shipping container he is pointing at says **Property of Brazil**, across the side. "No Brazil or Vietnam coffee is in the order that is leaving today."

The operator checks his clipboard and replies, "Huh, you're right. Number BRAZ7677324 isn't on any orders. How did the container even get to this port?"

"You got me," replied the representative. Then he sped walked over to the group of other countries' ICO members, looking panicked. "The Brazilians know what we're doing," he said to the group.

"What? How? Nobody has said a word. This is our first shipment for this deal!" replied Peru.

"I have no idea how they found out, but it's a clear message. The Brazilians have the largest port in this part of the world. Port Santos. There is no reason for them to have shipped a container to Veracruz.

Especially one that isn't even on an order! It's a rogue container!"

"Okay, relax," said the Rwanda representative. "There is no way they know. It has to be a mix-up. A coincidence."

"I don't know," said the Mexican rep, shaking his head. "These guys play dirty. You should have seen the way those damn Sicilians came at us after the council meeting. They are savages."

There is a moment of silence.

"Well, there is nothing we can do but keep our promise on the deal with our importers and hope the Brazilians, and especially the Scilians, don't find out," said Uganda.

"Importers," said Mexico, sarcastically. "We only have ONE importer! We just began and they *already* found out." The Mexican representative is rapidly pacing, with sweat dripping from his brow.

"Well, so what if they know?" asked Rwanda. "If they know, they will lower their prices to match ours. We will just have to undercut their prices. Then it's just about who can last the longest at that profit margin. But we have more countries on our side and better beans. We'll surely outlast them".

Mexico paces to the Rwanda rep and heatedly says, "It's not just about outlasting. It's about survival. Our *lives*. This isn't just business. Don't you know what the Sicilians are capable of?! The mafia has no moral compass. They will act in inhumane ways to get what they want! They will KILL to get what they want".

There is another moment of silence until the Peruvian representative speaks up. "Is it racist to assume they are in the mafia?" he asked.

"Well, if it is. Call me a racist," said the Mexican rep. "These guys are definitely mafia. No normal Sicilians are interested in coffee farming. No normal PEOPLE act the way they do – have the temper they do."

"I don't know…" responded Rwanda. "I think the normal Sicilian is pretty hot-headed."

"That's definitely racist," responded Peru.

The Mexican representative angrily storms off, frustrated that his business partners think this is a joke. *This is* no *joke*, he thought.

This is life or death.

Chapter 10

The Note Taker

Sal, Joe, and Tony are standing in a circle in a small, dark room. There is a wretched stench of body odor hanging in the air. The type of odor that only comes from nervous sweats. In the center of the circle formed by the three Sicilians, is a small, wooden chair on the verge of breaking from the weight it is holding.

“Aw shit, Tone! You’re gettin’ my shoes wet. Careful with that!” yelled Joe.

Tony has an empty gallon-sized metal bucket in his hands. Although empty, the bucket has water dripping down the sides. He turns, bumping into Joe because of the tight space in which they are confined. Tony turns on the faucet behind him, begins filling the bucket, and pointedly says “Oh shut the fuck up, Joe. It’s been a while since I’ve done this! You think you can do betta?”

Joe shrugs this off and doesn’t reply. He hates doing this work, so he is happy Tony volunteered. In Joe’s eyes, it always seemed barbaric.

Tony turns back to the chair, with a full bucket of water. He began pouring once more. As he does this, a low, muffled shriek fills the tight, dark room.

Tony is waterboarding the Rwandan ICO representative.

As he pours water out of the bucket, it hits the saran wrap covering the victim’s face and bounces onto Joe’s shoes once more. This time, Joe refrains from saying anything. Again, he hates doing this work. Thank god for his older brother.

The Rwandan has his hands and feet hog-tied around the back of the chair so tight he lost feeling in them thirty minutes ago. He vehemently shakes his head trying to avoid the water, as Tony is halfway through emptying the bucket once more. After a few seconds, he realizes the shaking is futile, and begins violently thrusting his body side-to-side, hoping maybe he'll push the chair over. Or break it. Anything to get out from under the water.

Eventually, he knocks himself over and falls to the right, bouncing his head off the ground. He tried to catch himself instinctually, but the damn hog-ties prevented him from protecting his damn self. This made him scream even louder.

"Shit!" yelled Joe.

"Why you bein' an idiot?!" yelled Tony. You're just makin' it worse for yourself!" Then Tony cocks his left leg and kicks the victim squarely in the ribs.

The room is filled with a loud crack – presumably his ribs – and then another shriek. The shrieks are growing louder and louder.

“Alright, alright, Tone. Time to let him speak again. Don't kill him before we can get answers now,” said Sal.

Tony bends over and thrusts the victim's chair upward. He does this so aggressively, the chair does a complete one-eighty, and instead of the chair landing on its four legs, it lands on the left side. The victim’s shoulder smashed into the ground and his head bounces off the floor once more. Another blood-curdling shriek fills the room; however, this one is quieter. It sounds exhausted.

“Tone!” Sal yelled. “Easy. We need answers. Not another dead body!”

Tony shakes his head at this, clearly annoyed with having a backseat driver during his torture session. More gently, Tony lifts the chair upright and places it on all fours.

“There you go, Princess. All better?” Tony asked, sarcastically.

The victim's chest was expanding and contracting rapidly, but now that the chair is on all fours, his chest is slowing. His breathing becomes less labored. Still far from normal, but better.

Tony deems him in good enough shape for a round of questioning. He rips the saran wrap off the Rwandan representative's face and yells, "You guys went rogue, didn't you?! Behind the ICO's back! Behind OUR back! Admit it!"

"Of course not," replied the victim in a hurried, broken manner. His breathing is still labored, making any form of communication difficult. "I don't know what you heard from Brazil, but the nation of Rwanda – and all the others for that matter – would never go against the ICO. Never go against our member countries."

Tony curls his hands into tight fists, turning red in the face. The Rwandan sees this and tightens his body, in anticipation of a slap, or a punch.

"I'll give you one last chance before we go back to the water park. Give us the name of the importer you're working with, and we'll spare you. We'll spare your partners."

"We have no such deal with any importers. We abide by the rules set forth by the ICO." Under his breath, he adds, "Unlike you three…"

Tony lets his right fist fly and lands it promptly on the Rwandan's nose. The chair tips backward and he once more, bounces his head off the concrete floor. There is no shriek this time. It would take too much energy, and he has none left. Just the whimper of a broken man.

Sal sighs, pulls out a cigarette, and lights it. He's been in these situations too many times in his life. He knows how it goes. It's a dance between the torturer and the victim. The victim doesn't want to give up info, the torturer gets mad and beats him or her. They do this dance for sometimes five minutes, other times five hours, and then finally the victim gives in. He always wondered why they don't just give up before the beating. Nobody has ever out-lasted the aggressors. Even if they did, they'd just wind up dead anyway. To Sal, it seemed like giving the info before the beating is just best for everyone. Except for the Companies that make torture equipment, he supposed. *They would want the victim to get tortured.*

This time, Joe walks over to tilt the chair upright, as he sees Tony is in no state of mind to do this guy any favors. There is a moment of silence, as the victim takes a beat to catch his breath and whereabouts again.

"Fine," he replied, still under labored breathing. "The contract you heard about from the Brazilians, or wherever you heard it, is true."

"And the name of the importer? Sounds like you smart guys were only able to land one contract. Hope it was worth it," Tony said.

"Mattingly–" the victim stops mid-sentence and spits blood on the concrete floor, "and Sons, Inc."

Joe hurriedly writes this down on a small notepad he pulled out of his jacket pocket.

Tony looks at Joe, who gives him a nod.

Sal, halfway through his cigarette, starts clapping. "Well done. Well done. You know, you would have saved yourself a lot of trouble if you'd have just given us the name in the first place. Then you could have avoided the water, the bangin' your head on the ground, and the burn mark on your neck."

The victim replied, "What burn ma–" then let out another shriek, this one just as loud as the first, as Sal put his cigarette out on his neck.

"Boys, you're with me," he said as he walked out the door.

"What about the ties?" asked Tony.

Sal takes a beat to think about this and replies, "Undo his feet, keep his hands."

Tony snorts from laughter at this and does as he is bid. *I wish I could where this bastard goes with a chair attached to him*, he thought.

Here's what happened. In early January, on their last two days in Palermo, the Brazilians told them about the deal Rwanda and the other smaller coffee-producing countries had with an unnamed importer. They decided it was best to leave a day early and make a pit stop in Rwanda to take care of business. Their families were none too happy that they got one less day with them, but hey, business is business. And while they loved spending time with their family, they *loved* business.

1

The day after the torture session, the Sicilians arrived in Ho Chi Minh City by plane. It was time they visited the best damn coffee farm operators in the eastern hemisphere. Shit, maybe in the world. *Probably* in the world.

The three of them decided it would be fun to surprise Nick and Gio. The boys thought Tony, Joe, and their father were going straight to Hanoi to continue their dealings with the politicians. However, after seeing their families in Palermo, the three of them agreed it was only right to see the remainder of their family before they got back to work. Joe and Tony really began thinking of Gio and Nick as their own family. Sure they were a pain in the ass sometimes, but what family isn't? Besides, Joe always wanted a younger brother. Now he has two.

The three Sicilians and Binh pull up to the Palermo Coffee Company and begin walking toward the front door where Gio and Nick have been staying since Tony ended the life of Nam Le.

Sal raps on the door, and smiles, thinking about the surprised look on his kid's face when they see him. However, it was Sal who expressed a surprised look when the door opened.

Standing in the doorway on the coffee farm they own all the way across the world in Vietnam, is Sofia. Sal can't quite wrap his head around what he is seeing. Sofia, expecting Liem with their food order, turns red when she sees Sal.

"Sofia," he said. "What– How–"

Nick, hearing his father's voice coming from the front door, gets off the couch and sprints to Sofia. He appears behind Sofia and gently scoots her out of the doorway. "Pop. What are you doing here? It's great to see you! I'm just surprised you guys are here. I thought you were heading back to Hanoi."

"We were, but figured we'd surprise you guys. But apparently, we're the ones who are surprised."

They share a moment of awkward silence, processing what is happening. Finally, Sal asks, "May we come in?"

"Yes! Yes, of course," Nick said, gesturing for them to come inside.

The three Sicilians enter, but Binh stays outside to find and catch up with Liem.

When they walk into the small space, they see Gio taking a nap on the couch. "Think I should wake him?" Sal asked Nick. "I know you guys have been bustin' your ass out here I don't wanna wake him if he's tryin' to catch up on rest."

"He's fine," Nick replied, lightly smacking Gio's cheek until his eyes fluttered open. Then his eyes grew wide.

"Dad!" Gio said. "What are you and the guys doing here? I mean, I'm so happy to see you! I'm just a little surprised. I thought you were going back to Hanoi."

Tony looks at Joe and says, “I got Déjà vu.”

“I’m surprised you know what that means, Tone.” Joe replied, sarcastically.

“Just wanted to surprise ya,” said Sal.

Gio smiles, still unsure if he is dreaming or not.

Sal looks at Gio and Nick, and says, “We know you guys have been workin’ hard and just wanted to stop by in person to say good job. We couldn’t have asked for a better duo to be runnin’ this farm.”

“Me and Joe could probably run it betta,” said Tony.

“You guys wanna stay here instead?” Sal asked, pointedly.

Joe laughs, hits Tony on the shoulder, and says, “Shut up Tone. I don’t wanna be stuck out here in the boonies. Seriously you two, great, great job. Everyone has been really impressed by your work. We’ve made sure Vinny knows about your efforts.”

This makes Gio and Nick blush a little, but they don’t want the guys to see, so they look down.

When their faces feel less warm, they look back up, smiling. “Thanks, guys. That means a lot,” said Nick.

“Yeah,” added Gio. “It hasn’t been easy but it's been a great experience.”

“Yeah, you even wasted your first reporter! Congrats!” said Tony, genuinely trying to be congratulatory. “Probably won’t be your last either. Reporters are always snoopin’ around shit they shouldn’t be snoopin’ in.”

Joe hits him on the shoulder again and gives him a stark look. When Tony sees the look on Gio’s face, it reminds him of the moment he ended a life for the first time. Tony’s first kill was when he was twenty-two – older than both Gio and Nick. He remembers how horrible he felt. It didn’t quite sink in for a few days after it happened, because the following forty-eight hours he was hopped up on adrenaline, caffeine, and cigarettes. But once he came down, boy oh boy, did he come down.

“Shit, sorry,” Tony said. “No time for jokes. But you guys really are doing a kick-ass job. It is not going unnoticed. Promise.”

This lightens up Gio's face a bit.

Joe walks over to the kitchen island (if you even can call it that, it's really just a small piece of plywood on a couple of two-by-fours), and points to a stack of papers. "What's this?" he said. "Someone writin' a play?"

"Oh, that's mine," said Sofia, embarrassed. "I'm writing a book, so those are my notes. I usually use my laptop but I forgot my charger and didn't wanna wait till I got home because I was afraid I'd lose my train of thought."

This news causes everyone to take pause. Finally, Joe breaks the silence.

"Sal, Tone, Nick. A word?" said Joe, heading into the bedroom.

Sofia gives Gio a look that says 'Am I in trouble?'. Gio reads this perfectly and just shrugs.

When they all arrive in the bedroom Joe starts without hesitation. "Look. Nick. You guys have been doing a terrific job here, really. We couldn't be happier. But we got an issue."

"Oh relax, Joe," said Tony. "It's just a book."

“It’s not just a book. I saw a few of the notes. She's writing about her experience here. The last thing we need is this operation becoming documented.”

Nick’s face turns paper white. He starts, “She’s not writing about anything illegal we’ve done. Really not even much about the operation. She's just writing about traveling and experiences and her–”

“Enough,” said Sal, sternly, putting his hand up. “Joe’s right. We can’t have anything documented remotely related to this operation. Even the papers in the kitchen are too much. She’ll need to burn them. She’ll also need to go home, son. This is no place for anyone outside of the family.”

He starts again, “But– She’s not outside the family she–”

“She’s not *in* the family. Ergo, she's *outside* of the family. She's a loved one. There’s a difference. You’ll eventually learn that we don’t tell our loved ones about the nitty-gritty details of any job. We especially don’t let them come see it for themselves. You know why, son?”

Nick doesn’t say a word. He is so nervous, and embarrassed, he can’t speak. He just looks at his father, silently.

Sal continues, “Because, most of the people who know details, either have the risk of going to jail, or getting wasted.”

This makes Nick's stomach twist into a pretzel. The very thought of Sofia in jail, or worse, dead, makes him want to throw up on his father.

“She’ll have to go home, son. For her own good. We’re saying this because we deeply care about her, and want to keep her safe.”

Nick is on the verge of tears now. *How could I be so reckless?* He thinks. *Of course this is incredibly dangerous for her. I just put her at risk. Never again.* Finally, he gathers up enough courage to nod in agreement. She must go home. But maybe he’ll let her keep the book. She worked so hard on those notes, and burning them seems a little over the top. The two of them can keep a secret.

The men stay in a hotel in Ho Chi Minh City for that entire week to make sure Sofia gets home, and check in on how Nick and Gio are doing. The boys are running like a well-oiled machine. Joe, Tony, and Sal are admittedly impressed with how well they are handling the pressure. Especially given that this is their first assignment.

Throughout the week, Nick and Gio make a few comments about missing home. Missing their friends. Missing the Sicilian sunsets. Their hope is to put the bug in the family's ear that they have had enough. Of course, they can't just outright say they are tired of running the farm, especially not after they got in trouble for flying Sofia down here. No, they would stick the assignment out until their service is no longer required. No matter how long or strenuous.

The family could easily pick up on these hints and knew the kids were being pushed to their limits. But goddamn, they were impressed. They need help from the kids until the smaller countries are officially done fighting back.

Hopefully, their message to the Rwandan representative was the final pin in that.

After their week in Ho Chi Minh City, the men arrive in Hanoi. Time to meet with Duc and Dong to catch up on business. They once again find themselves in the smoked-filled office, with Dong sitting behind the desk and Duc sitting to the side. *The Robin to his Batman*, Joe thinks. *That is if Robin was ugly as fuck and never spoke. Except when he called us foreigners. Asshole.*

"Well, I think you'll find we put a good enough scare into those assholes. I don't think we need to worry about this up-and-coming wanna-be competitor Oligopoly any longer," said Sal.

"Oh? Then why is it that I just received pictures from one of our contacts, of our friends from Mexico, Peru, Uganda, and Burundi at the Port of Veracruz?" said Dong as he put a blown-up, pixelated picture on his desk to show the guys. "They clearly have shipping containers at the port too. You see that? 'Property of Peru,' it says. It appears you gentlemen scared the Rwandan representative, but that's about it."

"The rest are still moving forward with the deal," remarked Sal, dreamily, in disbelief.

"Don't matta," said Tony, waving off the picture. "We got the name of the importer. Let's just whack 'em. You can't sell coffee to a dead man."

"No, Tone. The answer to everything isn't 'let's just whack 'em.' We gotta be methodical about this. We're playin' chess here," said Joe.

"You know, *none* of this would have happened if you and Tone just stayed here over Christmas!" remarked Sal, facing Joe. "These other countries were able to form a coalition together because you two just *had* to go on fucking vacation!"

"How the fuck is this *our* fault, Sal?! We didn't know they were forming a rebellion. And you went back home too! Maybe it's YOUR fuckin' fault!"

Sal stands up so abruptly that he knocks his chair over. He grabs Joe by the collar and shakes him. "My fault?! I'm the only one in this group of assholes who makes smart decisions!"

Joe takes a deep breath to calm himself and replies, "Careful, Sal. When I'm the Don one day, you don't wanna be on my bad side."

"When YOU'RE the Don?!" Sal yelled. "You think Vin is gonna pass up someone who has been loyal to him for decades?! Someone who knows the Family and its dealings like the back of his hand?!"

"He would," replied Joe, still calm. "For his son."

Sal shakes Joe even harder this time until Dong breaks it up.

"ENOUGH!" exclaimed Dong. "Not in my office! This is a place of *business*. We don't discuss our emotions, like a bunch of assholes! *Sit*, Mr. Conti!"

Sal cools off and sits back down in his chair. The room takes a beat, and Sal is the first to speak again. "Tony's right," he said bluntly.

Tony, ecstatic, puts his hand to his ear as if to help his hearing. “What’s that, old man Conti? Can you say that once more?!”

“Fuck off, Tone. You’re right, and I admit it. We need to waste the buyer.”

“I believe he is right as well,” said Dong, as Duc nods in agreement. “We need to put a final nail in the coffin with this. We’ve risked too much. We need a permanent solution. What is more permanent than death?”

Duc speaks to the Sicilians for the first time in what has to be months. They almost forgot what his voice sounds like. “Dong. I agree we need a permanent solution, but should we perhaps bring it up to the ICO council first? We have a meeting in March. Perhaps we will discuss the matter then?”

Dong looks questioningly at Duc. “Discuss what? Are you proposing we complain to the ICO that the smaller countries have created an Oligopoly, after we ourselves, did so as well?”

"Well, I think it's important that our constituents know we are at least attempting to play fair and– "

Dong cuts in. "I think playing fair is out of the question at this point, Duc. Everyone knows we have gone against the ICO, our constituents included. Reporters from around the world are talking about how corrupt the coffee industry has become. No. The best thing for our constituents, for us, and for our business partners is to win. Playing nice is out of the question. We're in too deep. Crushing out competition is the only thing that will keep us afloat."

Duc nods to this and says. "Okay. Let's end it once and for all then."

"Great," said Joe, sarcastically. "But what about the exporting countries? What happens when they just find a new buyer?"

Tony smiles and lets out a small chuckle. "I got an idea for that too. Leave that to your older brother."

Everyone in the room sets their eyes on Tony as his small smile turns into a wide, evil villain's grin. *What could he have up his sleeve*? Joe wonders.

Chapter 11

White Powder

It's the first week of March, on a brisk, early morning in Palermo. Three Sicilian men arrive at a private airport. No, they are not Tony, Joe, and Sal. Although, they are friends of Tony. All three of them were once in the Italian Air Force but were arrested for improper use of aircraft. You see, the three of them were childhood friends. During grade school, they loved going to the A.C. Milan football games together. Especially when they played Inter Milan. What a rivalry that was.

They used to get their faces painted together and try to be the loudest ones in the crowd. As the saying goes, if you were the loudest, you were the proudest. And by god, they wanted to be the proudest.

One fateful night at a match versus Inter Milan, they started a thirty-person brawl. One man even died. The poor guy wasn't involved in the fighting, he just got trampled by so many people, he broke four ribs, which punctured his lungs, and he died two days later in the hospital. They felt pretty torn up about it, but he was an Inter Milan fan, so not that torn up.

On a different night, years later when they were in the Air Force and each about six Aperol Spritz's deep, they came up with possibly the greatest idea of all time. They decided they were going to steal three fighter jets and fly them directly over the Intern Milan stadium during a match. I mean, if they have credentials, it's not *really* stealing.

Plus their boss was an A.C. Milan fan, so surely he would understand. Find it funny, even. When you're six Aperol Spritz's deep, you can justify damn near anything.

So that night, they stole three fighter jets without the knowledge of the Air Force and flew over San Siro stadium. They got so close to the stadium, it shook. The goalie literally shat his pants. That made the pilots happy when they found out about it later.

Of course, you can't steal a fighter jet, fly it so close to a stadium it shakes, and make a goalie crap himself, without going to jail. So, off to jail, they went. The police decided it best to lock them up in Sicily to keep these guys as far away from Milan as possible. Shit, if Siberia was within their jurisdiction, they would have sent them there.

That is how Tony met these pilots. They became buddies because he overheard them telling their story to other inmates, and he thought it was just fantastic. Funny, even. They would eat lunch together, and they told him how they would be hard-pressed to ever find a job again. He assumed this was true, but Tony knew *he* would be able to hire them one day. He just didn't know when.

Today was that day.

They entered three jets the Sicilians rented for them at a private Palermo airport. They typed the coordinates Tony sent them in their GPS systems, and took off. First stop: Rwanda. Even though Rwanda gave up on their rebellion, the Sicilians figured they'd still hit them where it hurt once more. Make *sure* it was over.

The early morning is beautiful for the pilots. The sun is just beginning to rise and add some orange to an already colorful pink and soft blue sky. As they approach the first set of coordinates, they get into a V formation. Ten seconds later, the back doors of the plane open, and a sheet of white powder goes pouring out into the cotton candy sky. It is Arsenic Acid Powder.

The powder travels forty thousand feet down until it reaches land. It covers coffee cherry shrubs, machinery, and the skin of workers placing coffee cherries in buckets. The workers look up, confused about the strange white powder falling from the sky. Looking up was a big mistake. In a matter of seconds, the worker's eyes, skin, and lungs begin itching. Then burning. Then downright feeling like they're on fire. They begin running around the farm in chaos, unsure where to go to avoid the powder or how to make the burning stop. The crops are now coated with a thin film of white powder, almost instantaneously turning the dark green shrub, into a wilted, brown corpse.

The proprietor of the farm sees this from his office and doesn't move. He sits there at his desk, staring out the window, trying to understand what is going on. Although he doesn't know what the white powder is, he knows exactly who is responsible. His nation's ICO officials made it abundantly clear.

The pilots continue on their way to the next set of coordinates with the back doors of the planes closed, and only one-fifth of their white powder missing.

Next stop, Burundi. Then a few more before their last stop in Mexico.

1

Meanwhile, at the Port of Veracruz, it was just another day for Carlos Martinez. Carlos was a crane operator at the Port who loved his job dearly. To him, there was nothing like waking up early and working on the most beautiful Port in the world during sunrise.

He noticed this morning was a particularly beautiful one. One of those days that makes you appreciate your job even more than usual. And for Carlos, that's saying something because he already loved it so.

He began checking the shipping container numbers, verifying that the order was on his clipboards, then one-by-one placing them on the cargo ship. Now, Carlos has been working at the Port for a long time and has come to know a lot of the names on the shipping containers. However, one of the containers caught his eye. On it was the name of an exporter he didn't recognize. It read **Property of**

the Palermo Coffee Company. *Huh*, he thought. *Must be a new coffee company that is exporting. Although how can they afford their own shipping containers? Typically, they are only used for massive companies shipping massive quantities. Or co-ops.*

He checked his clipboard, and there it was on the order sheet. "The Palermo Coffee Company. Shipping one container," he read to himself. *They paid for it, so what do I know*? He thought, moving the crane to pick up the container, then placing it right next to ones that read **Property of Mexico**, **Property of Peru**, **Property of Burundi**, and **Property of Uganda**.

After some time, Carlos finishes up all the orders that are getting shipped on this vehicle and moves on to the next. The ship remains parked at the port as the crew prepares to take off, but little do they know, they will not be taking off.

As the pilots are flying to Mexico, they see an orange glow on the southeastern coast, then a dark gray and black plum. It's an explosion.

Right on time, the leading pilot thinks, grinning.

The explosion was so powerful that it did not just take out the shipping containers of the Sicilian rivals, it took down the whole goddamn ship. It even blew back Carlos's hair (however faint, as he was balding). Carlos jumps out of the crane he is working in, and sprints full force to get help. Although nobody will be able to help. The ship was halfway underwater in a matter of seconds.

2

That same morning, Sal, Tony, and Joe were headed to London. In the air, Tony even saw what looked like fighter jets, a little bit ahead and above their plane. *I wonder if that's our guys*, he thought. "Hey Joe, you think those are our guys?" Tony asked while pointing in the direction of the planes.

"No, dumbass. Our guys are going south. We're going north. You see the issue with your logic?"

"Yeah, yeah," replied Tony. He really thought it could be their guys.

Once they touched down in London, it was business for the three of them. They got in one cab and took it thirty minutes from the airport to the Mattingly & Sons, Inc. headquarters. Now, Tony wasn't the best with words. That's why, anytime there was a meeting that required negotiation or strategy, Tony typically kept his mouth shut, and let Joe and Sal do the bulk of the work; however, when it came to meetings that required, shall we say, Old School Mafioso shit, Tony was the man in charge.

For this meeting, Tony was the man in charge.

They step out of the cab, in front of a two-story gray building with a sign made out of thin canvas stretched on the front, above the front doors that read, *Mattingly & Sons, Incorporated. Circa 2023*.

In disbelief, Joe remarks, "The fuck is this? *This* is the importer? You gotta be kiddin'."

As he says this, one of the cords holding the top right corner of the sign snaps and the sign folds in on itself.

Tony snorts a laugh. “This is gonna be even more fun than I imagined,” and walks toward the front door with Sal and Joe behind him.

When they enter, there is a front desk, but nobody at it. It appears to have been vacant for some time. On the desk, there is no computer, no pen or paper. Not even a chair. Just dust settling quietly.

They continue through the entrance of the building and come across a stairwell. There is a sign on the wall next to the door to the staircase that says *Mattingly & Sons, Inc. – Suite 204*. Tony points to it and says, “The whole fuckin’ building is empty except for these guys? You’d think they were mobsters or some shit. I mean, what? Did they scare everyone else out of the building?”

Joe and Sal exchange an uneasy look and follow Tony through the door and up the stairs. They head down the second floor hallway, and when they reach the door for unit 204, Tony reaches for the doorknob. Joe grabs his shoulder before he can twist the knob, which startles Tony a bit. “What? What? What’s wrong Joe?”

"I think we just need to prepare ourselves for any situation." Joe puts his hand on the pistol in the waist of his pants.

"What?" replied Tony. "You think these guys are *actually* mobsters?" Tony snorts another laugh.

"Remember the building in Florence we had for two years? We scared everyone out of that building. This buildin' looks pretty fuckin' empty," Joe retorted.

"Yeah but Joe, that had like ten units. It was a tiny building. This is a two-story building with like thirty units per floor. No way that could scare *that* many people out of a building. They wouldn't want that many people to know, anyway."

"All I'm saying is… be ready for anything. We don't know what we're walkin' into. We couldn't find anything on these guys, remember?"

Tony frowns as he thinks about this idea. "Yeah, I rememba." He mimics Joe and grasps the handles of his pistol, ready for anything.

He gives Sal and Joe a nod that says, *ready?* They give him an affirming nod back, and Tony opens the door gently with the gun still hidden under his shirt.

When they enter the suite, all they see are fluorescent lights and white cubicles. The lights are blinding. Even worse, the light is bouncing off the pearl-white cubicles, making them seem even brighter.

They take two steps in slowly, and are startled when a young man, about twenty years old by the looks of it, stands upright abruptly in the middle of the cubicle maze. The kid's skin is pale and his bright red hair is in disarray.

"You the Son in Mattingly & Sons, Inc.?" asked Tony.

"Who's asking?" the kid replied.

"I'm fuckin' askin'," replied Tony. "Are you affiliated with Mattingly & Sons?"

Before the kid can reply, a middle-aged gentleman, with equally bright red hair walks out of what appears to be the bathroom, and into the bright white cubicle maze.

"Can I help you?" he asked.

"Yeah," replied Tony. "Are you, or this puny-ass fire crotch, affiliated with Mattingly & Sons, Incorporated?"

"Who would like to know?" he asked.

"Jesus, you're like an older, uglier version of this one," said Tony as he pointed to the kid. "*I* would like to know. And I think it would be very unwise of you to make me ask a third time."

The kid and the father look at each other for a few seconds and don't say anything.

"Okay, what the fuck. You two are really gettin' on my nerves. Is there anyone else I can speak to regarding Mattingly & S–"

Before Tony can finish his sentence, the younger man quickly drops down beneath the cubicle wall, and the older man pulls a pistol out of a holster on his waist and opens fire. Joe and Sal, who were behind Tony when the shots were fired, dropped abruptly to the ground and army-crawled behind a cubicle wall. Tony ducks, pulls a gun out of his waist as three bullets whiz past his chest, and drops to the ground, laying on his back.

He opens fire and lands a bullet on the kneecap of the older gentleman, who also drops to the ground.

Tony swiftly crawls over to the cubicle wall with Joe and Sal. Joe loudly whispers, "Tone! You're bleedin'!"

Tony looks down and sees blood spilling from his left thigh. Now he is wondering if he dropped to the ground voluntarily or not. He can't remember.

"I'm okay," he says calmly. He takes his shirt off and tightly wraps it around the hole in his leg to stop the bleeding. Then amazingly, he stands up in a crouch position and peaks out to find the red-heads.

They are nowhere in sight, but there is a trail of blood going back into the bathroom. "Alright. I'm gonna finish off Poppa red-head. Can you two take care of the kid?"

"You got it, Tone, I'll waste him," replied Joe as he pulled the gun out of his pants.

Joe and Tony stay crouching, and head in the same direction, and then split when there is an opening in the cubicle maze, Joe heads into the maze, and Tony heads to the bathroom.

Joe crouch-walks down the first aisle of cubicles slowly, leading with his gun. Nothing in the first aisle. He goes down the second, even more slowly this time. He has a feeling the kid is in this aisle, but again, nothing. *Shit, I hope he's not headed for Sal*, he thinks. *Then again, if the kid wastes Sal, he's probably doin' me a favor*. Joe smiles at this thought and starts down the third aisle.

The kid is cowering under a desk in the third aisle, waiting for Joe to cross him. It feels like an eternity has gone by for him as Joe walked the first couple of aisles. Finally, he can hear his footsteps approaching. Barely, but he can hear them. Then slowly, he sees the tip of Joe's gun come into sight, pointing down the aisle. The kid sees his opportunity. He closes his eyes, pulls the trigger tightly and unloads a round. He started shooting too early though, because all he did was shoot Joe's gun clean out of his hand. The kid opens his eyes, expecting to see a half-missing face staring at him, but instead sees a pistol laying on the floor in front of him.

Joe dives under the desk next to the young man, waiting for him to make the next move, but neither one budges. They hear the front door open, and someone in the room yells, “Who are you?! What did you do to my nephew?!”

Then, they hear gunshots coming from the direction of the front door where Sal is still crouched. It startles the young man, and he dives out from under the desk, pulling his trigger tightly and rapidly at the desk the big-nosed Sicilian dove under. Joe closes his eyes, expecting multiple shots to the face and chest. He opens his eyes after three seconds and notices he’s dry. No blood. No holes. *The kid’s outta bullets*, he thought, grinning. Then, Joe dives for the young man, tackling him to the ground. They hear five more bullets come from the bathroom as they are wrestling, but this time it doesn’t scare the kid. His adrenaline is rushing like a river after a rainstorm. They spend a mere ten seconds struggling with each other before Joe reaches for his gun on the ground, grabs it, and puts it to the kids' forehead. Without hesitation, he pulls the trigger. Dark red blood explodes from the kid's head and splashes Joe in the flash like a sadistic water balloon.

Joe, still on top of the young man, feels a hand on his shoulder and spins around swiftly, pointing the gun at the man towering over him. It's Tony. Joe relaxes and throws the gun to his side.

"I know why *I'm* covered in blood. Why are *you* covered in blood?" Joe asked. Before Tony can answer, Sal runs over to them, with blood on his shirt. Tony turns to Sal. "Why are YOU covered in blood?"

"Well, someone came runnin' into the room waving a gun around asking who I was and what I did with his nephew. So I took care of it." Sal looks down at his shirt. "Shit. I loved this shirt too. Loro Piana, you know. Bastard."

Tony replies, "Yeah, no kiddin'. I took care of old redhead in the bathroom. Looks like you took care of young redhead, Joe."

"Yeah," he replied. "Kid was definitely not a wrestler."

Tony chuckles at this. "Neither are you, wise-ass."

"Whateva, I took care of it," he said, gesturing to the headless young man on the floor. "How's the leg, Tone?"

"It hurts like a bitch. Think I need a docta?"

"What are you a fuckin' idiot?" asked Sal. "You gonna go to the doctor and tell them 'hi, we're in the Mafia, and just killed three people who were in a different Mafia. Please make my booboo feel better.' "

"I think this is a little more than a booboo, Sal!" said Tony.

"Relax. I got it," replied Sal. He then kneels by Tony's thigh and unties the shirt wrapped around it. "Unbutton your pants, Tone."

"You gonna suck his dick or somethin' Sal?" asked Joe, as Tony does as he is bid.

"Funny. Very funny," replied Sal. He then pulls a pocket knife out of his shirt pocket.

"Whoa whoa whoa. What the fuck you think your gonna do with that?" asked Tony.

"I'm getting the bullet out. Once we do that, we can wrap it properly."

Tony grimaces, prepping for the pain that is about to come. Joe turns away, but then sees the beheaded kid, and decides that's worse.

"Joe, break that glass case on the wall and get the first aid kit out. I need to wrap this right after," said Sal.

"On it," replied Joe, quickly.

When Joe comes back with the first aid kit Sal digs the knife in Tony's thigh. He let out a loud, deep howl of a scream as Sal dug around in his open wound. After just a split second, there is a clinking noise on the ground that sounds like metal on ceramic. The bullet came out.

"Damn. That didn't feel good," said Tony.

"Imagine doing it to your own leg," replied Sal, wrapping Tony's leg tightly with thick layers of gauze.

Sal's phone buzzes, and he checks who is calling. It's Nick and Gio. "Shit, I gotta take this. One sec." He stops wrapping Tony's leg and answers his phone. Tony finishes the job for him.

"Hey, boys! How's it going?"

Nick replies, "Good, Dad. Do you have a minute to chat?"

"Uhh, I'm kinda in the middle of somethin'. Is everything alright?"

"Yeah, yeah. Everything is fine. Just call back when you have time for a quick chat."

"Okay. You sure everything is alright? You sound worried."

"Yeah, everything is alright! Just wanted to get your thoughts on something. It can wait though."

"Got it. I'll call you tonight then. Seeya."

"Bye, Dad."

Sal hangs up and says, "Alright, let's clean this shit up quickly and get back to the hotel. I gotta call the kids back." The remainder of their day is spent hiding the bodies and cleaning the surfaces they may have touched. Good thing there weren't many.

3

The next morning, Sal is in his boxers and an undershirt, pacing nervously in his hotel room in Hanoi. He is on the phone. "Hey, sorry boys. Me and the guys had a situation in London we had to deal with. What'd you wanna talk about?" He's nervous because the last thing they need is something to go awry at the farm. Also, because after Binh picked them up from the airport, he went out and they haven't seen him since. Granted, it's only been one night. But Sal was worried about Binh. Not worried because they need him for translating and for driving them around, but because Sal knew the pain Binh had gone through early in his life. Boy, did he know. He also knew that Joe and Tony are growing more and more suspicious of Binh. A disappearance is the last thing he needed.

"London?" asked Nick and Gio in unison.

"The fuck you doin' in London? They don't grow coffee," said Nick.

"Watch your mouth. And that's right. They don't. But they import coffee. That's where the Mattingly & Sons, Inc. headquarters was."

"Was?"

"Was," replied Sal. "They seemed to have some kinda dealin's with the gangs in London. But we ended that."

"London has gangs?" asked Gio.

"Everywhere has gangs. It's just that none operate as well as Cosa Nostra," Sal said, proudly.

They all share a small laugh at this. "Enough about me," Sal said. "What'd you boys wanna talk about?"

There is a beat of silence on the other end. Sal can tell they are nervous to say what is on their minds.

Nick starts. "As you know, we've been operating the farm for a while now–"

"Doin' a helluva job too," added Sal.

"Thanks, Dad. Well, it's been quite some time. And you initially said it'd only be probably a month or two. We were just wondering when a more permanent operator was going to take over. We have the farm in a great spot. It's pretty much self-sufficient now. It just needs someone to take care of miscellaneous paperwork. We don't want to sound like we're complaining or trying to rush you or the operation, it's just that it's been a while and we were hoping to get experience with the family in other areas that–"

"Enough," said Sal. There is a moment of silence that gives Nick and Gio queasy stomachs. "I suppose you're right. We haven't prioritized getting a permanent fixture in that position. That's on us. It's just you boys were doing so well, and we had so much other shit to take care of these past six, seven months." Sal takes a big breath and releases a long sigh.

"So… you think we'll find a permanent operator?" asked Gio.

"Yeah, Son. We'll prioritize it too. Promise. Let me talk with our contacts in Hanoi and see if we can have someone sent over soon."

Nick and Gio quietly fist bump in celebration of hearing this. “Thanks, Dad.”

“You got it. I’ll talk with our guys tomorrow and keep you updated. Love you both.”

“Love you too,” they say in unison, and hang up.

Chapter 12

The Alfa Romeo

Two days after Sal's phone call with his kids, he hears a door slam loudly, and a thud that awakens him at five in the morning. The sound came from the room next door. Binh's room. Sal was worried sick about Binh the past two days. Joe and Tony were growing angry that their chauffeur was missing. They had to take Ubers everywhere, which was normally fine, but they could never remember the damn exchange rate. It wasn't a money issue, it's just that it made them feel stupid. And they don't like feeling stupid. Plus, conventional money has a paper trail. It's important to the Family that you leave as little of a monetary paper trail as possible on every project. Each Uber ride was another step closer to global law enforcement putting them behind bars in whichever country wanted them the most. Oh, and the small talk. If they had to listen to another Uber driver ramble on in a language they couldn't understand, they were gonna kill somebody. And it would probably be their next Uber driver.

Sal runs out of his room, to the one next door. He entered the room swiftly, and panicked, just to see a grown man on his back, laughing hysterically.

"Binh," Sal said. "What's so funny? And where the hell have you been?"

Binh can't stop laughing to answer his question.

"Did you fall?" asked Sal.

Binh nods, still laughing uncontrollably.

"Look, Binh. I went out on a limb for you when I hired you for this project. Please don't make me regret that decision."

Sal is still standing over Binh, who is on the ground, now just giggling.

Sal continues. "Joe and Tony are growing wary of you. They are not too fond of your drinking habits. To be frank, neither am I. I know you've had a hard life. I know. I was there with you for the hardest parts, for God's sake. But this is unacceptable. You need to get a handle on things. Your father wouldn't have wanted to see you like this."

This makes Binh stop laughing immediately. Instead, he's on the ground, straight-faced. Then after a few seconds of silence, Binh becomes watery-eyed.

Sal, unsure what to do says, "Just bein' honest, old friend. I'm tryin' to help, but only you can get yourself outta this rut." Then he turns around, and walks out of the room, leaving Binh on the ground piss-drunk and near-sobbing over the memory of his father, and the horrible, wretched way he died. Or more accurately, was murdered.

1

That same morning, just outside Ho Chi Minh City at the Palermo Coffee Company, Nick and Gio hear a knock on the door. "That must be him!" exclaimed Gio. The place is tidied up and their bags are packed.

In the two days between now and the conversation they had with their father about wanting to find a permanent operator for the farm, Sal granted their wish. Well, really it was Dong who granted Sal's wish. You see, Sal called the officials asking for help finding a permanent operator, especially someone they could trust. The officials reached out to Lan Nguyen, the gentleman who owns the second largest farm in Vietnam with whom they have a partnership. Coming from a long line of descendants of farmers, Lan was very connected to the agriculture community in Vietnam. Dong called up Lan that very day and tasked him with creating a list of options for taking over the largest coffee farm in Vietnam. Lan mentioned he had a cousin who was a rice farmer who might be interested in selling his farm if he received an above-market-value price for it. Dong and Duc were hesitant to pay an above-market-price for a shitty rice paddy, but Sal reminded them they owed the family a favor, after all the bullshit they had to deal with in regards to poisoning the farms, handling the Mattingly & Sons debacle, and so on. All said and done, The Vietnamese government ended up buying the rice farm for ten percent over market value and sending Lan's cousin to operate the Palermo Coffee Company.

They let him inside, showed him around, took him on a tour of the farm, and gave him the low down on payroll and taxes. Then just like that, Liem was driving them to the Ho Chi Minh City airport.

Sal decided it was time the boys took a trip home. Joe and Tony were actually okay with it because they themselves hadn't been away from Sicily as long as these young boys had. What they weren't okay with, was that Sal was going with them. The Conti's agreed the boys would fly out of

Ho Chi Minh City, Sal out of Hanoi, and they would meet in Catania.

This made Joe lose his cool. He and Sal got into a screaming match about how Sal *just* went home. He didn't need to go back. If he went back, Joe and Tony should go back. Sal sourly disagreed. He figured if Joe had two sons helping in an operation for the Family, that he didn't get to spend quality time with for six months, he'd feel different. But alas, this was not the reality. Joe tried to forbid Sal from going home, saying that when he became the Don he would make Sal's life a living hell. This made Sal want to go even more.

Besides, Sal had other plans he had to tend to while back in Palermo.

Secret plans.

They ended up agreeing that Tony and Joe would go back after the Conti's trip. Everyone decided it best to have someone in Vietnam to hold down the fort and make sure another competitor Oligopoly didn't form. And Joe sure as hell wasn't going to leave that responsibility up to Tony himself. Therefore, Joe stayed.

2

When Nick and Gio's plane touched down in Catania, they were acting like kids in a candy store. They are rambling on about what they should do first, where they should go, who they should see. They are the youngest, and loudest people in first class. People begin staring. But the boys don't care. If these normies had any idea of what they went through the past six months, they'd understand their excitement to be home.

The boys find a gentleman in a tophat with their names on a sign, who takes their bags. They follow him out of the airport. "Remind me, how long of a drive is it back to Palermo?" asked Gio.

"Two and a half hours to the house," Nick answered. "Why?"

"Ugh. I'm tired of sitting. Why don't we ever fly directly into Palermo?"

Nick sighs. "I dunno. Dad says it's cheaper to go to Catania."

Gio sighs in return. “For a buncha rich guys, they sure can be cheap sometimes.”

Nick laughs at this. “Hey, at least they put us up in first class.”

Gio smiles in return. They exit the airport and head toward the car that will drive them two hours home, where they will meet up with their father.

After a grueling two-and-a-half hours of the driver's bad music and cheesy podcasts, they finally arrive home. The two young men walk to the front door, and Nick pulls out his keys to unlock it. He slides the key into the hole and turns it. Before he opens the door, he gives Gio a look of concern.

“What?” Gio asked.

“The door. It was unlocked. Didn’t Dad say he would be coming in after us?”

Gio turns pale when he processes what Nick is saying. “You think someone is in there?”

“I dunno. One way to find out,” he replied.

“Wait!” said Gio in a hushed but stern voice. “Should we get a weapon?”

Nick looks around and picks up a palm-sized rock. “This will have to do.”

Gio picks up one and gives Nick a nod to enter the house. Nick slowly turns the door and they enter. Immediately, they are immersed in the overwhelming, mouth-watering aroma of a Bolognese sauce, and pop music. They exchange a confused look and walk into the kitchen, where the smell and music are coming from. When they enter the kitchen they see the back of what they would assume is a beautiful woman, with long dark hair.

“Sofia?” says Nick, still holding the rock above his head.

The woman turns around. “Oh! Hey boys! What do you think?” she asked with a big smile on her face. “Why are you holding rocks?”

“What do I think?!” replied Nick. “I think you scared the shit outta us. That’s what I think.”

Gio drops the rock and runs over to the pot with the Bolognese simmering, taking a big inhale.

Sofia chuckles, puts her arms around Nick’s neck, and says, “I wanted to surprise you two!”

"Well, surprise you did," said Nick laughing. He then plants a big kiss on her lips, and Gio makes a gagging noise directed toward them.

"What, you don't like the sauce?" asked Nick sarcastically.

Then they hear footsteps in the foyer. "Hello?" said a voice coming from the direction of the steps.

All three of them turn serious, as they know Sal wasn't supposed to be home for another two hours. Gio picks the rock back up and cowers behind the kitchen counter. Nick picks his rock up as well, standing in front of Sofia.

Sal walks into the Kitchen.

"You gonna hit me with that fuckin rock, Son?" Sal said to Nick, smiling.

Nick and Gio simultaneously drop their rocks and smile back. "Dad! I thought you were coming in a few hours after us!" exclaimed Gio.

"Yeah I was, but I saw there was an earlier flight leaving, and I was able to transfer my ticket to catch the plane. I guess I was a little excited to be back home with my boys. And of course you, beautiful Sofia," he said nodding to Sofia. Then he takes a big whiff of the air, and his eyes grow big. "What do you guys have cookin' up in here?!"

"Oh, I started a Bolognese. I wanted to surprise you guys when you got home," said Sofia.

Sal looks at Nick and says, "Don't ever let her go."

Nick kisses Sofia on the cheek. "Never," he said.

"Wait, how'd you get in the house, Sofia?" asked Sal.

"No offense Sal, but the key-under-the-doormat trick is older than Egypt."

Sal laughs. "Yeah, yeah. I guess so. Well, I'm gonna drop my bags off in my room. I'll be back down. Nick and Gio, you left your bags outside on the porch. Might wanna get those."

"Shit, that's right!" said Gio running outside to grab the bags.

As Sal drops his bags off in his room, he decides to make a call.

He dials a number, and hits "Call". The phone rings once, and then a man with a deep, hoarse voice answers. "Sal! How's it going, my guy?"

"Good, good. How you doin' Dom?"

"Ah you know, can't complain."

"Stayin' outta trouble?" Sal asked.

"Yeah, no jail time for me these days. Just time with my wife and kiddos."

"Good. Family is important," said Sal.

"The *most* important," said Dom. Then there was a pause in the conversation. "What can I do for you, Sal? Somethin' you wanna talk about?"

"I gotta favor to ask. It's a big one."

"It's not gonna end with me in jail, is it?"

"No, no. It'll be discrete. It's a sure thing."

"What is it?"

"I need a car bomb planted. The target is a red 1962 Alfa Romeo."

"Doesn't sound all that discrete," said Dom, pointedly.

"It's low risk, Dom. Promise. I have the garage code where the car stays. The owner is away, his family is out during the day. It'll be quick and easy."

"No way I'm doin' this during the day. I don't need people seeing me go into a stranger's garage a few days, or worse, *hours* before their car explodes. Also, how do you have the garage code? Is this someone you know personally?" Another pause on both sides. "Sal?" asked Dom.

"It's Giuseppe DiGrasso," he answered quickly, trying to rip off the band-aid.

"Oh, Sal. What the fuck. Vinny's kid? I would rather have trouble with the police than trouble with the family. And aren't you still working for the family?"

"Yeah, yeah. Don't worry about trouble with the family." Now, Sal likes to think of himself as an honest man, but what he says next might be the biggest lie he's ever told. "Vinny knows about the bomb. It was his idea."

Dom sighs. "Trying to off his own Son, huh? That's barbaric."

"Yeah. It's complicated but necessary. Vinny is willing to pay very, very handsomely."

"Well… the kids are lookin' at Colleges now, and goddamn they are expensive. How handsomely?"

"*Very* handsomely," replied Sal.

After a couple of seconds, Dom replies, "You got it, Sal. I owe you one anyway. You've always had my back."

"Thanks, Dom. We really appreciate it."

"Of course, even though I owe you one, I still expect this handsome payment."

Sal chuckles. "We're good for it, Dom. Don't worry. You'll get your money. Guaranteed."

Later that night, Gio, Nick, Sofia, and Sal stuff their bellies with Sofia's Bolognese. After Sal and Gio go to bed, Nick and Sofia stay up a little longer to talk, just like when they first started dating.

"It was a great idea for you guys to stay here with your Dad while you're back in town," she said. "I'm sure he misses spending quality time with you two."

"Yeah. We miss it too. We've missed a lot of things," Nick said while staring deeply into Sofia's dark, mysterious eyes.

"I know the feeling," she said, staring back into his equally dark eyes.

"How about I take you out while we're back? Some place nice."

"I would love that!" Sofia said, excitedly. "We can get dressed up, order champagne, and celebrate you being home."

"Good idea! We should go in style. You know the Don's son? Giuseppe?" asked Nick.

"Yeah, what about him?"

"He has this beautiful car. A cherry red, '62 Alfa Romeo. Joe and I got pretty close during the operation – bonded over great cars. He mentioned I could borrow the car if we ever wanted it for a night on the town, so long as he wasn't planning on taking it out. He's still in Vietnam so he definitely won't be using it anytime soon. Maybe I'll call him tomorrow and see if he'll let us take it out this weekend for date night."

"Ooooo! A red Alfa Romeo? Hot car!" she exclaimed. "You really think he'd let us use it?"

"Doesn't hurt to ask," said Nick. Then he leans in for a kiss.

"Wanna watch a movie?" asked Sofia.

"Sure. Watcha feel like watchin'?"

"Hmmm, Gone With The Wind? You know I love those American classics."

Nick scoffs. "Ah, Sof, those American 'classics' are ass. You don't wanna watch something more modern? Or something less… American?"

Sofia doesn't say anything. She just looks at Nick, knowing he'll cave.

"Alright, fine!" Nick said, smiling. Gone With The Wind it is, even though we've seen it a million times.

Sofia smiles as she gets up to grab the remote. "I think we bought it on Amazon sometime last year, didn't we?"

"Probably," said Nick. "If not, let's just buy it. God knows we watch it at least once a year."

Sofia chuckles and lays down on the couch, pulling Nick down by the arm to lie behind her. She buys the movie and clicks "Play" on the screen. No more than ten minutes in, they are both asleep, breathing heavily and slowly. Some say people sleep better when they are near their loved ones at night. I suppose they are right. They slept soundly as ever.

3

That very night, Dom drives over to Giuseppe's villa in Palermo, dressed in all black. It was a good thing he was doing this at night. He realized he knew this neighborhood pretty well, and would stick out like a sore thumb in this young, fit neighborhood the DiGrasso's live in. Dom stands at about six foot four inches tall, weighing nearly two-hundred and forty pounds. He is built like an NFL linebacker, just with more of a gut and less muscle.

He parks about eight doors down from Giuseppe's villa and walks down the sidewalk toward the house quickly. The backpack strapped to his gargantuan shoulders whips violently from left to right. *Better not upset the bomb*, he thought and slowed down until the backpack stayed put on his shoulders.

Finally, he reached the garage and entered the code. Once the door was about two feet off the ground, he stopped the door. It was louder than expected, and he didn't want to risk the noise waking up anyone in the house. He then takes the backpack off and barely squeezes under the door. When he sees the Alfa Romeo, it hypnotizes him. Dom has always been a car guy, and sometimes a beautiful, classic car like this stops him right in his tracks. He shakes his head. *Alright, quickly*, he thought. *In and out, just like the old days*. He slides under the car and gets to work. No more than sixty seconds later, he slides out of the car and exits the garage. *Easiest cash I've made in a while*, he thinks, smiling. As he's walking back to his car, he realizes he forgot to close the garage door. *Shit!* He thought. *I can't leave that door open two feet. It'll be obvious someone was in there.* He begins lightly running back to close the door. He hates going back to the scene of the crime – there is too much room for error. Too much risk of someone catching you on the second trip back. He reaches the garage door, and quickly types in the code. The door begins moving up, instead of down. *Shit! Fuck!* Dom thinks and starts panicking, worried the noise will wake someone up. After what feels like an eternity, he punches in the code again, and this time it goes down. Dom decides he's been here far too long, and takes off down the sidewalk in a full sprint. When he gets back to his car, he looks in the rearview mirror. No lights are on, nobody is outside. He's in the clear. He takes a few deep breaths and drives back home.

4

The next morning, Nick calls Joe. While it's ringing, Nick looks at his watch. *Eight AM,* he thinks. *So it should be one in the afternoon in Hanoi. Yeah, he should be available.*The phone keeps ringing. On the last ring, Joe picks up.

"Nick! How are things back home?"

"Hey, Joe. Things are good. Sofia surprised us with some Bolognese right when we got back."

"Don't ever lose her," Joe said.

Nick chuckles, “Yeah yeah. I won’t. Hey, I had a question for you.”

“What’s up?” asked Joe.

“I remember you offering up your ‘62 Romeo for when I wanted to take Sofia out someplace nice, and well, I was hoping to take her out this weekend. We haven’t had much romance the past nine, ten months, and I was just hopin’ to make her feel special, and since you’re still in Hanoi I assumed you wouldn’t be using it anytime soon so I–”

“Nick,” said Joe. “You’re rambling. Take the car. Enjoy your time with her.”

“Thank you! Thank you, Joe! We really appreciate it.”

“No problem. I remember when Josephine and I started dating and I was always out on jobs. It can be hard to keep the romance alive. And I only had one to three months long assignments. I couldn’t imagine doing one as long as you and Gio have at your age.”

“Thanks again, Joe.”

"You got it. I'll tell Jo you're coming to the house Saturday night, to make sure she's there to let you in and give you the keys."

"Sounds good, I'll be there at eight," said Nick.

"Cool. I'll let her know. Enjoy date night."

"Thanks," Nick replied. Then they both hung up.

"Who was that?" asked Tony. He and Joe are sitting on a patio, eating lunch.

"Nick. He's borrowing the Romeo to take Sofia out."

"Shit. You're letting him borrow your car? You don't even let me borrow your car."

"That's because you're a shit driver," said Joe.

"How do you know Nick isn't a shit driver? You never even seen him drive!"

"He's responsible. Being a good driver is just about being responsible – which you are not."

Tony snorts a laugh. "Yeah, whateva."

That weekend, on Saturday at eight o'clock on the dot, Nick shows up at the DiGrasso's villa. He raps on the door.

"Hey, young man!" Josephine exclaims as she answers the door.

"Hi, Mrs. DiGrasso."

"Please. Call me Josephine. You look handsome." she said smiling.

"Thanks, Josephine," he said, smiling and slightly embarrassed. It was hard for him to call someone so much older by their first name. His parents drilled it into him that you always address your elders by Mr. or Mrs. – never their first name. It seemed antiquated to him now, but sometimes it's hard to get out of a habit.

"Come on in. The keys are on the kitchen counter. I made some Arancini if you want a little bite to eat before you head out."

"Ah, no thanks. I better not. Smells delicious though." Nick walks to the kitchen counter, finds the keys, and heads to the garage.

“Thanks again, Mrs. DiGrasso!” he said as he entered the garage.

From in the kitchen, Josephine yelled, “Please! Call me Josephine! Enjoy your night!”

Nick smiles and closes the door to the garage behind him. He takes a second to admire the Alfa Romeo. It hypnotizes Nick the same way it hypnotized Dom a few days earlier. He takes a deep breath and enters the car. He is surprised to find that he’s a little nervous. He hasn’t taken Sophia out on a date in almost a year. He’s worried he forgot how to be a gentleman; how to make her feel special. As he keeps being reminded: he can’t lose her. Plus, he has big plans tonight. Plans she doesn’t know about quite yet, which makes him nervous. But he knows she loves him, as he loves her.

He sits in the driver’s seat, and puts a hand in his pocket, feeling the smooth gold ring holding a sharp, hard diamond he put in his pocket before he left. He takes a few more seconds to reminisce on the first couple of dates he and Sofia ever had. The sunsets they would watch together on the beach.

Little does he know, these are the last thoughts he will ever have.

He takes another deep breath and slides the key into the engine. The very second he turns the keys, he hears three clicks, and the car erupts into fire.

Chapter 13

Don't Blink Twice

"No, Pops," said Joe. "The ICO isn't even holding meetings anymore. Even the smaller countries have left and are trying to do their own thing– "

"Which they can't! We took care of the smaller countries too, Pops!" Tony cuts in.

"We've rendered the ICO powerless."

It's early morning in Hanoi, just hours after the Romeo blew up. Joe and Tony are FaceTiming their dad from their hotel room, while Vinny is sitting poolside, smoking a cigar and drinking a glass of Brandy. Hey, don't judge Vinny for drinking in the morning. It's *late* morning in Palermo. Besides, he's basically retired.

"That is fantastic, boys! Hah! You've really outdone yourselves with this operation," said Vinny.

"Yeah, Dad. I think we're even gonna take a trip home soon. Things are pretty self-sufficient out here at this point. Old man Sal doesn't wanna leave it alone quite yet so we agreed to wait until April when he gets back to Hanoi, and then we'll come back and can tell you more about it in person."

"Yeah, about that," said Vinny, hesitantly. This makes Joe and Tony exchange a look of concern. "Sal's not going back to Hanoi."

"What! Why not?!" asked Joe, almost panicked.

"Someone killed his boy. Someone killed Nick."

"Oh Jesus Christ," said Tony. "Who would go after Nick but not me, Joe, or Sal? Not that I want someone to come after us, but still. Doesn't make sense."

"Well… that's the other thing. They were going after you, Joe."

"What? How can you tell?" he asked.

"Because they blew up the Romeo, while Nick was in it. They were going after you."

Joe and Tony become silent on the other line. Joe gets a notification on his phone while they are on FaceTime. It's a text from Josephine that says exactly what Vinny just said.

Vinny continues, "We're still trying to figure out who did it. Might be retaliation from those Mattingly & Sons, guys. Or maybe a crew from one of the smaller coffee-growing countries. Sal is convinced it's Mattingly & Sons."

"No. It wasn't them, Pops," said Joe.

"What? How do you know that?" asked Vinny.

"Because it was Sal."

"Wow. That's a big accusation son. Why do you think Sal would ever betray the Family like that?"

"Because he knows I'm gonna take over as the Don when you step down. But if I'm outta the picture, it's he who gets the job. Who else could get into my garage without breaking in? I just received a text from Josephine. She said there were no broken windows in the house. Not even signs of a break-in on the garage door! Whoever did it, knew the garage code!"

Tony adds, "You know what? Sal and Joe got into a screaming match before the Conti's left for Palermo. I've never seen Sal give anyone the look he gave Joe. I thought he was gonna kill him right then and there."

Before Vinny can respond Joe continues, "His judgment has been impaired lately too. I mean, fuckin' Binh. The raging alcoholic. Sal told us he 'owes him one'. The fuck could that be about? You know why Sal could be in debt to a Vietnamese alcoholic?"

Vinny says, “No. I do not. And Joe, your garage door was in pretty bad shape from the bomb. I’m not so sure you’d be able to objectively tell if there were signs of forced entry from it.” Vinny sighs. “I don’t know this Binh, guy. He’s really that bad?”

“Yeah, Dad,” Tony adds. “I can even attest to that. He’s that bad. He’s untrustworthy.”

There is another moment of silence. Finally, Vinny says, “Let me talk to Sal. He is one of my oldest friends. One of my most trusted advisors. I’ll be able to see through any bullshit if there is any.”

After they hang up, Vinny goes into his contacts and searches for Nicolette DiGrasso, his long-lost daughter. He stares at his phone screen, nervous. His thumb hovers over the “Call” button, and then swiftly he exits out of his contacts, going back to the home screen. *Not yet*, he thinks.

1

In the following days after the Romeo blew up, Sofia, Gio, and Sal didn’t leave each other's side. They were grieving together. They found the grieving process to be more tolerable with loved ones around. Especially if the loved ones were grieving the same loss you were. There is something about community, and about sharing feelings with others that can't be expressed in words, that makes the grieving process a little easier.

Not easy, just easier.

Vinny calls Sal twice during the week after, but both times it goes straight to voicemail. After the second time, he stops calling. Giving Sal some space and time to grieve is probably for the best right now. He wouldn't be able to have serious, educated dialogue anyway in this state of mind.

Sophia spent many of her evenings on the beach with Gio, remembering what it was like when Nick was there. How much fun the three of them had on the beach, watching the sunset. Sal never tagged along for the beach during that week. In those hours, he stayed at home and prayed to his sweet Teresa up in heaven. He prayed that Teresa and Nick were reunited, and supposed they were. He was a little jealous of Nick, getting to be with his sweet Teresa.

She was the best damn woman. She made Sal feel on top of the world. He knew it wasn't his time quite yet though – he had to take care of Gio. Make sure he becomes a self-sufficient man. He supposed Gio was pretty much there though. He handled the job with the family in Vietnam very well.

The guilt started eating him alive. *He* killed his son. *He* killed Nick. Sure, he didn't plant the bomb, but he ordered it to be done. He lost his appetite, and ten pounds to go along with it. This really concerned Gio and Sofia. They understood his suffering but had no idea about the guilt he was experiencing. Had no idea it was he, Sal, who accidentally killed his son, Nick.

Finally, after a week Sal decided it was time to reach back out to Vinny. He knew Vin would be worried about him, but he just didn't think he could talk about it then. Now, he felt ready.

Sal drives over to Vinny's villa, to see him in person. He figured this was an in-person conversation.

When he arrives, he raps on the thick, white marble door. The door seemed different today – ominous. Almost as if it had something it wanted to say to Sal. Something to warn him about. After a while, it opens, and Julia is standing in the doorway.

She sees Sal and gives him a sympathetic look. "Hey Sal," she said, without her usual pep.

"Hey, Julia. Just wanted to see Vin. Catch up."

"Of course, come in," she said, gesturing for him to enter. "He's out back, by the pool. Can I get you anything? Cigar? Brandy? Water?"

"I'll take a scotch if you have it."

"One scotch, coming up," she said, smiling.

Sal walks over to the bar, as she pours one. He picks it up, throws it back, and puts it back on the counter. They exchange a look of sorrow, and Julia fills it up once more. This time, Sal just takes a sip and walks to the back patio to be with Vinny.

From inside, Julia watches the two men greet each other and embrace in a long hug. She decides it best to leave them alone and heads upstairs.

Once they let go of the hug, Vinny says, "Sal… words won't do it justice, but I am so sorry for your loss. How have you been handling it?"

Sal throws back the rest of his scotch for the second time and takes his time figuring out a response. Vinny saw this and figured it said enough.

"Why don't we go downstairs, old friend? Have a quiet conversation?" Vinny asked.

Sal nods in agreement, and the two of them head inside and down the stairs. Vinny's basement is extraordinarily spacious, and low-lit. He always felt a basement should have a somber feel. There is a floor-to-ceiling wine rack on one wall, filled with expensive bottles. To the right of that, is a large white marble bar with open shelves behind it stocked full of brandy, gin, amaretto, and sambuca. In the middle of the room, is a poker table with eight chairs at it, and a pool table with gold legs. In just about every corner, there is a white marble statue of a baby with wings. Those always gave Sal the creeps. He figured they were supposed to be angels, but every time he saw them he felt as if he was staring at the devil himself.

Vinny grabs a bottle of sambuca and two glasses. He points to the poker table, and Sal takes a seat in one of the chairs. Vinny follows suit, then pours two fingers of sambuca into each glass. They sit there, just looking at each other for thirty seconds. Vinny takes a sip of sambuca, smacks his lips, and asks, “So really, Sal. How are you doing?”

“Not good, Vin. Losing Teresa, and then two years later losing my boy… a man should never have to experience those two things. Especially so close together.”

Vinny nods along, frowning and staring at his drink.

Sal continues, “He was finally makin’ a name for himself. When he was a boy, he always asked to be in the Family. Become a businessman. Of course, he was too young. But when his opportunity came… boy did he shine.”

“He did fine work, Sal. You should be proud,” replied Vinny, somberly.

Sal nods, not looking up from his drink. "You should have seen the ring."

Vinny gives Sal a questioning look. "What ring?" he asked.

"Sofia's ring. Well, Nick's ring that he was going to give to Sofia. An engagement ring." Sal exhales a big sigh and says, "He was gonna propose that night. I remember before he left, he was so nervous. He showed me the ring, but I could hardly see it because his hands were shakin' so bad." Sal lets out a small nostalgic chuckle. "Then he got into his car and drove off. I had no clue he was going to Joe's house first to pick up the Romeo."

Vinny raises his eyebrow at this comment. "Would it have made a difference if you knew he was going to my son's house first?"

"Well, no. Whaddya mean, Vin?"

"I mean, would you have told Nick not to go if you knew he was taking my son's car? Did you know someone was after Joe? Have any hunch at all?"

"No, no. Of course not. I woulda told you immediately. No."

Vinny nods at this. They share a moment of silence, and each takes another sip of their drink.

"Sal, I've been thinking. After Teresa passed, you didn't take time off. In fact, you worked harder than ever before. I didn't think it was possible, you already worked harder than anyone I knew."

"It's all that kept me sane, Vin," Sal said in agreement.

"I get that. But now, I think you should take some time. My boys are in Vietnam, they can handle it. I want you to have some personal space for a while. Time to reflect."

Sal looks up from his glass and into Vinny's eyes. "Where is this coming from, Vin?"

"Coming from my heart. I'm worried about you."

"When Teresa passed, you were the one who encouraged me to dive deeper into my work. Why are you pushing me away now?"

"I'm not pushing you away, Sal. I just think… my boys are worried this might be too much to handle. That it may be impairing your judgment. Making you more… emotional than usual."

"The fuck is that supposed to mean, emotional? This was Joe's idea, wasn't it? Gettin' me out of the family?"

"You're not out of the family, Sal. Just taking time off."

Sal shakes his head in disbelief. "You really think I'd make emotional decisions? I'm all business. Always have been."

"Well, the boys think you've been making emotional decisions for some time now, and that this would just… exacerbate it."

"When? When have I EVER made an emotional decision, Vin?" Sal asks, heatedly.

"They are under the impression–"

Sal slams the rest of his Sambuca back,

"that Binh was an emotional hire. They told me you 'owed him one', or something of the sort. Now, that doesn't sound like a business decision to me," Vinny says calmly, pouring two more fingers of sambuca into Sal's glass.

"It was business, Vin. You can count on it" he said, taking a big gulp of his sambuca.

Vinny stares at his glass, deliberating Sal's words. "Sal, how do you know this guy?"

Sal remains quiet, also staring at his glass, then takes another gulp. "Our fathers–" he began, hoarsely slurring his words now. "They met each other when Cosa Nostra was heavily involved in the heroin distribution. If you remember, my father was in charge of the distribution in South East Asia. Binh's father was a linguist and knew just about every language spoken in that part of the world. Of course, my father needed a translator. He wanted to find *one* person who spoke *many* languages. The fewer people involved, the better, as you well know."

Vinny nods along in agreement and lets Sal continue.

"So, my father found Binh's father. At the time he was a professor at a University but was having a hard time relating to the next generation. He wanted to apply his knowledge in the real world, instead of teaching it to idiot kids. So, when my father approached him for some real-world work, he got pretty damn excited. He pounced on the opportunity. But being a translator for Cosa Nostra means seeing stuff most people don't ever see – don't *wanna* see. Binh's father was a straight arrow but had one weakness – a gambling problem. He was clearly uncomfortable with who he was working for, but my father doubled his salary from the University. I mean, shit, he had two kids and a wife to care for. Between the gambling debts and the responsibilities at home, he couldn't turn down the money."

Sal finishes off his sambuca, and Vinny immediately fills it back up.

Sal's words are getting more sloppy by the minute. "When I was eight years old, I loved Asia. It was this mystical place in the movies, and pictures I saw. So when I found out my dad was going to Vietnam on work trips, I *begged* him to take me with him. I just had to go. Finally, he caved and took me. They used to meet at our house if they were in Italy, or Binh's father's house if in Vietnam, to discuss business. Binh's mom passed away soon after he started doing work for my father, so they felt the Nguyen household was the safest place moving forward. They figured the kids weren't gonna be able to understand what they were talking about. That's how I met Binh. He'd come to my house in Sicily for the meetin's, and once his mother passed, I'd go to his house in Vietnam. We were the same age and became close. My father would take me to Vietnam twice a year to see my friend. We'd play in the basement while they were upstairs discussing things we thought were boring. Four years later, Cosa Nostra ended the vast majority of their dealings with South East Asia. My dad told me I wouldn't see Binh anymore. Couldn't write to him neither. I was heartbroken. We were best friends. Pen Pals. I convinced him to take me back one last time. I thought it was to say goodbye. Little did I know, he was going back to 'tie up loose ends' as you might say."

Sal's voice darkens, and the slurring worsens.

Binh and I were in the basement, playing as we did. We heard loud voices coming from upstairs. It sounded like our fathers were yelling. We walked up the steps, cracked the basement door open and peeked into the kitchen, where they would discuss business. My father was pointing something at him, and we heard Binh's father say 'please. I won't tell anyone anything. You have my word.' *Begging* my father for something. We couldn't figure out what he was begging for. Then we heard my father reply, 'Doesn't matter. You know too much. This is the way it has to be.' Then, my father shot him in the head and killed him. Turns out, the thing he was begging my father for… was mercy."

Sal looks down at his glass and a tear slowly rolls off his cheek, onto the poker table. Vinny is staring at Sal blank-faced, listening intently.

Shakily, he adds, "We were each just twelve years old. We saw my father end his father's life. I soon realized, my best friend would hate me forever." Sal slams the remainder of the Sambuca. "Binh had lost both parents by age twelve. He slowly slipped into the dark grasp of alcoholism as a *teenager*. I felt like it was my fault. I felt like I had to do anything I could to help him out. There wasn't much I could do, with him living in Hanoi and me living in Palermo, but once we planned this operation, I felt as though it was finally my time to help him out. Get him back on his feet."

Vinny empties his glass and stares at it. "Sal," he said looking up from his glass and into Sa's eyes. "Thank you for sharing that story with me. I had no idea."

Sal shrugs. "Anyway, that's how I know him. I think I need some water," he said standing, or more accurately, stumbling from his chair.

"Of course," Vinny replied. As they were about to walk up the stairs, Vinny turns around and faces Sal. "Sal, one more question. I just can't figure it out. Do you have any idea how that bomb got into Joe's car? Have you heard anything from the police investigation, or maybe anything from our sources within the Family? Anything at all?"

"Hmm, no. Why?" Sal said, blinking twice.

Vinny sees this and his face darkens. "Just hoping we can catch the bastard. For the both of us," he replied.

Sal nods in agreement and the two of them head upstairs for some water.

"I betta get goin'," Sal said after they finished two glasses of water in the kitchen.

"How you gettin' home Sal?"

"Well… I drove here, so probably my car," he replied.

"No, no. You're in no condition to drive. I'll go get Julia. Have her drive you home."

"Thanks, Vin. You've always looked after me. Like an older brother. I hope you know I do everythin' I can to return the favor to you," Sal replies. Then he turns around to fill up his glass with water for the third time.

Vinny doesn't reply. He just turns around and walks upstairs to get Julia.

"I give you all my loyalty!" yells a drunk Sal Conti, as Vinny disappears up the stairs. Then to himself, he whispers, "All my loyalty."

3

As soon as Sal and Julia leave, Vinny steps outside by the pool, lights a cigar, and FaceTimes Joe. He immediately picks up. He is in a hotel room with Tony.

"Jesus Christ. Don't you guys ever leave that fuckin' hotel room?" Vinny says.

"We got room service and free cable. What do we need to leave for?" replies Tony.

Vinny laughs and shakes his head. Then he gets serious. "Alright. I got big news for you boys."

Both of their faces get serious with him. "What is it, Pops?" Joe asks.

"You were right. You were right about Sal. It was him. It was FUCKIN' him!" he spat out, angrily.

"As in, it was Sal who planted the bomb in my fuckin' car?" asked Joe.

"Yes," Vinny answered, growing red in the face.

"How do you know? Who told you?" asked Tony.

"Sal."

"*Sal*? Sal told you?!" asked Tony.

"Yes. Well, indirectly. I got him three sheets to the wind and when I asked if he knew who planted the bomb, he said 'no' and blinked twice. That was his poker tell when he'd been drinkin'. I would know, I've played four hundred fuckin' hands with that bastard. So he knows who did it. It may not have been him directly, but his son's blood is on his hands somehow."

"Jesus Christ," said Joe. "I knew it! He wanted me outta the picture."

"Fuckin' wild," said Tony. "Well, whadda we gonna do about it? This can't go unpunished. As long as you are *sure* about this poker tell, Pops."

Joe cuts in, "Oh what are you talkin' about?! *You're* gonna say we have to be sure it was him? *You*? Of all people?! Mr. Fuckin' Trigger Happy?!"

Tony shrugs and doesn't say anything else.

Vinny calmly says, "I'm sure, Tone. I've never been more sure about anything in my life."

"So? What are we doin' about this Pops?" asked Joe.

“I already know how to handle it. But first, I need you two back in Sicily.”

Joe and Tony exchanged a look. A look that expressed a thousand emotions.

Chapter 14

The Jackson Pollock

It's a sunny April morning. Julia is outside, in their pool laying on an inflatable tanning bed in the water. Vinny is sitting in a lounge chair, smoking a cigar, and staring at his phone screen. He has Nicolette's contact pulled up once again. His thumb hovers over the "Call" button, but this time he builds up the courage to actually hit it. It rings, making Vinny's heart race. After two rings, it goes to voicemail. He looks at his phone, frowns, and hits the call button again. This time it goes to voicemail after only one ring. He frustratingly hits the button again, and it goes through immediately.

Nicolette picks up. "How the hell can you have three butt dials in a row?!" she says, angrily.

"Nicolette!" He says. "Hey, um, yeah those weren't butt dials. I was intentionally calling you."

"Why?" she asks.

"Just wanted to check in with my baby girl. See how things were going."

"Okay…" she says, clearly confused. "Things are good. April is kind of the last month until the American tourists flood the streets of Paris, so just trying to enjoy a little peace and quiet while we can."

"Paris? Oh fun, are you on holiday or something?"

"What? No. I live here, Dad."

"Oh… didn't like Siciliy anymore, huh?"

"Well, my fiancé lives here and we moved in together."

"Oh, yes. Your brother told me that you were getting married."

"Which one? Big nose or Big ego?"

"I think big nose and big ego describe both of your brothers," Vinny said chuckling. When he hears silence on the other end, he stops laughing immediately. "Um, well that's exciting! When is the big day?"

"June 18th."

"Ah, I see." There is a long pause on both ends. "Well, Nico, I know you didn't invite me or even tell me about the wedding for a reason… but, would you ever change your mind? I can't miss my baby girl's wedding."

"I'm not your baby girl. I invited Mom, and I don't want the day to be ruined. She'd be devastated if she saw you. And rightfully so. You treated her like shit, with your bimbos, never being around, always doing shady shit for the 'family'. You always knew how to please the 'family' but never knew how to please your *real* family. A bit ironic, don't you think?"

"I don't know if I'd call it ironic– "

"Sorry, Vincent. We've made up our minds."

"Nico. I know I wasn't a present father for you. I know I disrespected your mother. But please, if you could find it in your heart to invite your old man I would be so grateful. I've changed a lot, I swear. I'm a present and loyal partner, I have taken a step back from a lot of the responsibilities at work, and I am a good father to Joe and Tony. And would like to be a good father to you as well, if you'd consider it."

After a long pause, she says, "Okay. I'll think about it. I gotta go though. Pierre and I are late for our brunch."

"Okay, of course– " but before he can finish, she has already hung up.

Vinny puts his phone on his chest, covers his face with a fedora, and basks in the April Sicilian sun.

1

That same morning – of course, it wasn't morning in Hanoi – Joe and Tony were on their way to the airport to fly home. Binh is dropping them off in the black Escalade. They were excited to say goodbye to this asshole for good.

"You excited to see Jo and the girls?" Tony asked.

"Oh, you bet. Christmas feels like a lifetime ago. I think they'll be over the moon to hear we're back to stay for good. This operation has taken a toll on everyone."

"Especially Nick," said Tony.

"Yeah. Especially Nick," Joe agreed.

Tony asks, "What do you think you'll do first when we're b–" but stops speaking abruptly when Binh swerves aggressively out, and back into the lane.

"Binh! What the fuck, man!" yelled Joe.

"Sorry, sorry. All good," Binh replied, turning around to make the apology and slightly veering into the other lane again while doing so.

"Just watch the fuckin' road," Joe said.

Joe and Tony both sniff the air, trying to figure out what the acidic smell is they just got a whiff of. At the same time, they realize it was gin, coming from Binh's breath.

"What the fuck? Is that gin?" Joe mouthed to Tony.

Tony shrugs, and they both check their watch. One in the afternoon. Starting early even for Binh. They both decide to just remain quiet. They don't want any distractions for Binh if he is in fact drunk.

About three kilometers from the airport, they approach a stoplight. This is no ordinary approach though. They are just twenty yards from the stoplight and are still charging forward at eighty kilometers an hour. Joe and Tony exchange an 'oh shit' look.

"Binh! Binh!" yells Tony as they are approaching the red light. But it is too late. Tony looks to his right and sees lights approaching them at the same speed. They brace for impact. However, the driver of the car approaching them wasn't drunk like Binh, so he was able to make a concerted effort to stop his vehicle to avoid a catastrophic collision. It was a good effort but not quite enough to avoid a collision. The car t-bones the black Escalade, but only going about twenty kilometers per hour due to the opposing driver's coherence.

The black Escalade tail whips. Its back tires skid sideways from the collision, leaving black rubber marks on the road and smoke billowing from the back of the vehicle. It wasn't the worst collision ever, but it was enough to make their ears ring.

Tony looks at his hands, his arms, his legs. *They're all there*, he thinks. He still can't hear anything because his ears are still ringing, but he looks at Joe and sees he is trying to say something to him. All Tony can hear is a high-pitched ringing getting louder, and softer. Louder, and softer. He reads Joe's lips that are trying to say *let's get the fuck out* and decides that's a good idea.

Joe and Tony slide out of the car immediately. "We gotta get the fuck outta here, Joe," said Tony, who can finally hear his surroundings now that they are out of the car and on their feet.

"Yeah, last thing we need is the Hanoi authorities on our ass. I think we've pushed our luck here."

This time, Joe does a quick check to make sure nothing on his body is broken. Thankfully, nothing is broken. Neither one can believe they made it out without a scratch. Although the bullet hole in Tony's leg from the shootout with Mattingly & Sons is throbbing. *Oh well. I've had much, much worse*, he thinks. They give each other a thumbs up, and quickly get their bags out of the back, which was easy because the back window was shattered to bits from the collision.

The other driver involved slowly got out of his car and started heading toward the black Escalade to make sure everyone was okay. Except when Joe sees the man approaching, he takes off. Tony follows behind him.

"Where are we going?" asked Tony.

"To the fuckin' airport!" he replied.

"We're running?!"

"You got any better ideas?! It's only, what, three kilometers? Plus, we can't get in trouble with the authorities here for being involved with a drunk driver. We've come too far to risk it on some stupid shit like that!"

Tony stays quiet because he agrees. So they put their heads down, and run with their bags on their backs and suitcases dragging behind them. As they are running, they already hear sirens blaring, racing to the scene of the crash.

"What… about… Binh?" Tony asked. His breathing is becoming labored. This run is becoming damn near impossible for him. The gunshot wound in his leg feels like it has its own pulse. But he doesn't complain. Doesn't even slow down. "You think… he's… gonna get… in trouble?"

"Probably," replied Joe, breathing heavily but not as labored as Tony. "This… will be his third time… getting in trouble… for drunk driving. I don't know the rules here… but that can't… be good."

Tony realizes he feels for Binh a little bit. He remembers what it's like fucking up and going to jail. You wish you could go back in time – get a second chance to do it over. However, life doesn't work that way. You make a mistake, you have to live with it. But he also realized that you damn well better *learn* from it too. He figured if this was Binh's third time getting in trouble for drunk driving, he hasn't been learning from his mistakes.

Hopefully, this time is different.

Finally, they arrive at the airport sweaty as hell. "Ah, Joe," said Tony, still breathing rather heavily. "I haven't had swamp-ass this bad since '97."

"What happened in '97?" Joe asked.

"It was just a sweaty year for me."

Joe ignores this. "We should call Dad. Let him know we're on our way soon," he said, already dialing.

2

Vinny received this phone call just thirty minutes after he got off the phone with Nicolette. In between the calls with his children, Sal had come over to Vinny's villa for some brandy and conversation. Sal noticed that Vinny seemed a little off the past couple of weeks since their last conversation – more stoic. Kind of like the type of

Don you would read about in books and see in the movies. He was never like that. Vinny was always very loud, animated, and flamboyant. This new attitude was concerning Sal.

Vinny sees Joe is calling him and picks up on the last ring. "Boys!" he exclaimed. "You on your way home?"

Huh, seems like his normal self when he's talkin' to his kids, Sal thinks. But he supposed that's the nature of being a parent. There is nothing in this world that is better than hearing from your kids.

"Yeah, Dad," Joe replied.

"Why are you outta breath?"

"We had to run to the airport. We're in line at security right now."

"You *ran* to the airport? What happened to Binh dropping you off?"

Sal hears this, and his face turns pale. *What the fuck did Binh do?* he wondered.

"He was drunk. Got into an accident a few kilometers from the airport. We couldn't risk getting in trouble with the authorities by being associated with a drunk driver. Last thing we need is them digging up why a couple of Sicilians are in Hanoi."

"Agreed," replied Vinny.

"Well, we'll be there tonight. We were able to find a direct flight to Palermo. We'll come over as soon as we get in."

"Sounds good. Safe travels."

"Thanks, Pops. Bye."

They each hang up, and Vinny stares off into the sky, tanning on his lounge chair. Sal, who is on a lounge chair next to him asks, "Everything okay?"

"Your boy got them into an accident. They ran three kilometers to the airport."

"Oh, shit. Is everyone alright?"

"Tony and Joe are. Not sure about Binh. They took off before they could see how he was. I'm sure he's fine if the boys were able to run three kilometers afterward."

"Why did they run? Why didn't they just have someone drop them off?"

Vinny takes his sunglasses off and turns to Sal. "Because your boy was drunk driving. They didn't wanna wait around for another driver and risk gettin' in trouble with the authorities and having our history in Vietnam dug up." He puts his sunglasses back on and faces the sky again. "And rightfully so."

Sal doesn't say anything. His stomach turns to knots as he thinks about what could have happened if Joe and Tony had to speak with the authorities. The knots grow even larger when he thinks about what *is* going to happen to Binh. He knows this isn't the first time Binh's gotten in trouble for drunk driving. Thinking about all this makes Sal want to vomit. He chugs water from the bottle next to his chair, takes a sip of brandy, and faces the sky again.

3

As Tony and Joe are in the security check line at the Hanoi airport, they notice a few Vietnamese guys kitted out in dark green uniforms looking for something. It's the People's Public Security — the Vietnamese Police. Tony taps Joe on the shoulder and points in their direction. "You don't think they're looking for us do ya, Joe?" he asked.

Before Joe could answer, they make eye contact with the guys in green and see them start running. Joe and Tony look around, wondering if they are coming for them or someone else. They each individually deliberate running, but don't want to look suspicious if it isn't them who the police are running for. Plus, they are crammed tightly in the security check line. Finally, the guys in green reach Joe and Tony, yell a few words at them in Vietnamese and pull them out of line. Joe and Tony struggle with them, telling them to let go, but the guys in green are relentless. They slap handcuffs on the Sicilians, bring them out to their police vehicles, and push them in. A third officer throws their luggage in the trunk.

The car reeks of cigarette smoke, seemingly baked into the beige, leather upholstery. The smell is burning Tony's nostrils, scoring the hairs inside. *I knew I shoulda used that nose hair trimmer Joe's girls got me for Christmas*, he thinks. When they drive off, he turns to Joe and says, "Fuck, Joe. Where you think they're takin' us? We gotta be at Pop's house tonight!"

Joe checks his watch. "Shit. It's two o'clock here. That means it's already nine in the morning back home. Even if we get released tonight, and find another direct flight we won't get there until next morning."

"How long is the trip if we get a direct flight?" asked Tony.

"Fifteen hours," Joe replied.

Tony sat quietly for a second then said, "We better call Pops when we get the chance. We'll need a new game plan."

4

As the day goes by, Sal and Vinny barely exchange any words. After sunbathing, Vinny walks to the beach with Julia, leaving Sal alone in the big, empty house. They offered for him to join, but Sal declined. He's spent enough time in the sun. He said he'd better get home, but Vinny insisted he stayed and spent time relaxing. "We'll be back in no time, and then we can have dinner together," he told Sal, who conceded. He decided some quiet time would be good anyhow. Plus, it was nice Vinny wanted to spend time together again. It seemed to Sal that over the last week or so, something in their relationship had felt… off.

While Vinny and Julia were gone, he watched Gone With The Wind twice. He knew how Nick and Sofia loved that movie, and it made him think of his now-perished son. After the movie ended for the second time, he gets up to get some water and realizes there are two empty bottles of Chianti on the white marble coffee table. *Shit. Did I drink two bottles of wine by myself during that movie marathon?* He decides he did when he started feeling dizzy from standing up. It was so automatic, like blinking, or breathing, that he didn't even know he was drinking the bottles until the deed was done. There weren't even wine glasses around. He drank straight out of the bottle.

The two bottles of wine made him sleepy, so he decided to take a nap on the couch. He was so tired, not just because of the wine, but because ever since Nick died, his sleep has been riddled with nightmares. Nightmares of Sal killing his other son, Gio, with his bare hands. Choking him until the air entered his lungs no more. Sometimes it was even Sofia. He would wake up from these nightmares in a cold sweat, shaking from fear. Sometimes, he'd discover that he had been crying during his dark dreams. His face would be caked with salty tears and snot when he'd awaken.

The alcohol typically made his dreams worse, or at least more vivid. He knew this but he couldn't stop drinking. If he didn't have a drink or two, or ten, before bed he couldn't fall asleep. And he figured nightmare-infested sleep was better than no sleep. Although, he began questioning that logic after some time.

Gio and Sofia had no idea he had a drinking problem. Sofia had been staying with them since Nick's passing to help out around the house where she can, which they both greatly appreciated. It did, however, mean there was one more person in the house to catch on to Sal's new drinking habits. That part he didn't like.

Sal became brilliant at hiding it in plain sight. He'd put brandy in his morning coffee mug, with just a splash of coffee to mask the smell. He'd put sambuca in his water bottles when he would be doing anything outside. He'd even stashed a few flasks of scotch around the house in places they would never suspect, like under the vanity cabinet in the bathroom, or next to the shampoo bottles in his shower. They had no idea.

5

As Sal dozed off into his nap, Joe and Tony were fighting to get out of Vietnam, and back home. When the police cars finally arrived wherever they were going, they escorted the gentlemen out of the vehicle and into a dark, ominous building. This was no official police or governmental building; it looked like it hadn't been used in decades — centuries, even. They walk Joe and Tony down a hallway dimly lit by flickering lights and reeking of urine. They both have to hold their breath to avoid vomiting.

There are copious doors on either side, but they don't enter any until they reach the end of the hallway and open a door on their right.

They sit Joe and Tony at an aluminum table – hot from the overhead light blasting the metal. The three officers sit across from them. Nobody says a word for thirty seconds.

"Well?" asked Tony. "To what do we owe this tremendous pleasure?"

One of the officers replies in English, "Do either of you speak English?"

"Yeah," they both reply in English.

"Ugly fuckin' language though," Tony added,

The English-speaking officer chuckles and nods. "Well for this meeting, why don't we speak the ugly language? I'm afraid we are not well-versed in Italian."

They both nod in agreement.

"Great. I'm Officer Nguyen." He gestures to the men to his left. "This is Officer Dong and Officer Trang."

Joe replies, "Okay, Officer Nguyen. To what do we owe this gesture?"

"We received a call regarding an accident three kilometers south of the airport. Drunk driver. When we got there, we saw two gentlemen fleeing the scene. They looked an awful lot like you two," he replied, pointing at Joe and Tony across the table from him.

"We have pretty generic faces," said Tony. "How can you assume it was us?"

"Generic?" Officer Nguyen laughs. "Not generic in this country, Mr. DiGrasso."

Tony and Joe exchange a look of deep concern and unease.

"Ah. You boys are wondering how we know your names. Yes, yes. Understandable. Well, here's what happened." The Officer sits back, lights a cigarette, and starts. "When a coffee farmer by the name of Nam Le sold his farm, it took us by surprise," he said pointing to the other two Officers sitting by his side. "We knew Mr. Le… somewhat well. Knew his father started the farm, and grew it to be the largest one in our fine nation. We also knew Nam took over once his father passed away. They were both so passionate about the farm — it meant a great deal to that family." The other Officers nod in agreement. Tony and Joe wondered if they even knew what he was saying, or if they were just nodding because they were loyal henchmen. They supposed it could be either.

"Why would the People's Public Security have an interest in knowing coffee farmers?" asked Tony. "They doin' illegal shit at the farm?"

The officer replied, "That farm was — and still is — our largest source of tax revenue. We like to know where our money is coming from."

Tony's eyes grew wide.

The officer continues, "As I was saying, we were surprised to see he sold his pride and joy. A couple of weeks after the sale, we tried reaching out to see what he was up to – if he retired, started a new business, what have you – but got no reply. We come to find, Mr. Le went missing. So, we went digging."

"And what'd you find?" asked Joe.

“Yeah, you have us on the edge of our seats,” Tony followed up, sarcastically.

“We found a group of Sicilians making big purchases and investments in our nation's coffee industry. Then magically, an oligopoly appeared. New laws appeared in the agriculture industry. Small farmers just… vanished.”

The officer takes a beat then adds, “I know your name because it is my *business* to know your name. I know what you and your family have been up to.”

Joe and Tony’s faces harden.

There is a moment of silence

“Now honestly, these activities have bolstered our economy — increased our tax revenue, thus increasing my department's funding.”

“Wait. We weren’t cheatin’ on our taxes?” Tony asked looking at Joe,

“Of course not, Tone,” he replied, annoyed.

“Why not?! Why are we givin’ them the fruits of *our* labor, eh?!”

"Because," said Joe. "That's an unnecessary risk of getting caught. They got Capone for tax fraud."

"Yes, they did," agreed Officer Nguyen.

"Okay, so what?" asked Tony. "We in trouble or somethin'? Fuck that. I need my lawyer. I'm done talkin'."

"You're only in trouble if you don't cooperate," said the Officer.

"Cooperate with what?" asked Joe.

"Well, we could seize the land — since we have enough evidence to prove you took it illegally; however, we don't want to do that."

Joe and Tony exchange a confused, mysterious glance at each other.

The officer continues, "We wouldn't be able to maintain the farm as profitable as you men have. No. You've proven yourselves to be astute businessmen. Very resourceful, if I may say."

"Thank…you…?" said Tony, still confused. *Why are they complementing us now?* He started thinking.

"So no, we don't want to seize the land. Unless we have to, that is. We simply want a bigger piece of the pie. More than tax revenue. A royalty, if you will."

"The fuck?" said Tony.

"How much?" asked Joe.

Before the officer could reply Tony says, "Joe, you can't be serious. We can't give these guys a royalty! We already gave Duc and Dong a percentage and Pops was pissed at that!"

Joe stonewalls Tony and asks again, "How much?"

"Five percent of gross revenue," replied the Officer.

"FIVE PERCENT?" asked Tony, flabbergasted. "No way. Uh-uh. Pops would never allow this, Joe."

"Deal," replied Joe, calmly.

"WHAT THE FUCK, JOE?! No! No deal!" said Tony.

"Tone! Stop! Running the operation and giving away five percent is better than having *no* operation." Joe points to the officers sitting across the table. "He said it himself, they could seize the land if they damn well please. This way is a win-win."

The officer smiles. "Yes. A win-win."

"Officer," said Tony, flatly. "Would you be so kind as to give me and my brother a moment to discuss this preposterous deal?"

Officer Ngyuen stands up and replies, "Of course." He gestures for the other two to stand with him and they exit, leaving Joe and Tony still handcuffed in the poorly light, sadistic sauna that is the interrogation room.

Joe keeps staring across the table even though the seats are empty. Tony turns his whole torso to face Joe, stern and red-hot.

"LOOK AT ME!" yelled Tony, accidentally spitting a little on the side of Joe's face.

Joe slowly turns his head to face Tony. "I'm looking," he said.

"Not even gonna clear it with me before you make the decision, is that it?"

Joe keeps staring, silent.

"We're *partners*, Joe! We are *each* Capos! I am not your little bitch that will agree with whatever decision *you* wanna make. The decisions *we* make, together, are a reflection of the family. I'm not gonna let Pops believe this is an option *we* agreed on. It's unacceptable."

"Tone," Joe said calmly. "This is the *only* option. Whether we agree on it or not. Would you really rather go home, and tell Dad that the last *year* of work was wasted because you got sloppy and decided to kill the first person you laid eyes on in Vietnam?" Joe starts to grow louder as he speaks. "We can't keep losing out on business – backtracking – because you can't keep your cool!" These last few words, Joe damn-near yelled.

They both let their words sink in and just keep staring at each other.

"The issue with Nam worked out in the end," said Tony. We have the largest farm in Vietnam, and executed our mission."

"You're right. We did. But now we stand to lose it," replied Joe, in a staccato fashion. "I love you, Tone. And I respect you as a partner. But our hands are tied," Joe said, holding up his handcuffed hands and growing teary-eyed. "We have to take this deal. We can't fight back on this one. They have us cornered."

Tony nods, then hangs his head. Joe sees a tear fall from Tony's face. "I love you too, Joe. And I know you're right. You're always right. It's just hard for me to accept that we're in this situation because of me. Because of my hot head."

Joe says, "Hey, like you said earlier. We're *partners*. We get each other in bad situations, and we get each other out of bad situations. *Together*."

"Yeah well it feels like a whole lotta you Pops and ole' uptight ass Sal gettin' me outta these situations lately," replied Tony. He brings his head up to face Joe, and another tear falls from his eye.

"That's Family," said Joe, calmly again.

They both grow quiet and cool off. After ten minutes of silence, Tony walks over to the door and bangs his fists on it with his wrists still restricted in cuffs.

"We're ready!" he yelled out.

Seconds later, the three officers walk in again, and sit down across the table.

"So, gentlemen? Do we have a deal?" asked Officer Nguyen.

"Yeah. You have a deal," replied Tony.

"Excellent!" he said, standing up. "I'll have my office reach out to yours to set up details."

He gestures for the other two Officers to stand again, and they head for the door.

"Hey! You forgettin' somethin'?" asked Joe, holding up his handcuffed wrists.

"Ah! Yes, yes," said the officer, rummaging in his pocket for keys. Finally, he finds them and releases the Scilian's wrists. The three officers exit, leaving Joe and Tony in the room once again.

"Well," said Joe checking his watch. "That took a solid hour and a half outta our day. It's already three-thirty our time. We better call Dad and tell him we need a change of plans. No way we'll get to Palermo before midnight their time."

Tony has a devious smile growing on his face as Joe says this. "Hold off on that call to Dad, Joe. Let me make a few of my own calls first."

6

Only one hour later at four o'clock, Joe and Tony are in the air in an American Fighter Jet.

"How do you know these guys again, Tone?" asked Joe.

"You know those pilots that helped us drop the arsenic on the farms?" he asked.

"Yeah," replied Joe.

"Well, they had friends in the American Air Force based in Vietnam. They owed my buddies a favor for somethin' so they called it in. They said it should only be ten hours, at our speed. Palermo is five hours behind Hanoi so we should be in at…" Tony looks to the ceiling, thinking. "Nine in the evening Palermo time. "

Joe smiles wide. “I guess going to prison paid off,” he said as they glided through the air, going home for good.

7

Sal was jarred awake from his long nap when Vinny and Julia came back home. He sat upright and looked at his watch. It read nine o’clock. *Shit. Nine in the morning or evening?* He wondered. He peered out the windows and decided it was nine in the evening.

“Hungry?” asked Vinny.

“Starved,” Sal replied.

“Perfect, we got sandwiches from Bonducci’s,” Vinny said, holding up a bag and a six-pack of beer. “Let’s eat.”

Sal, Vinny, and Julia quietly sat around the kitchen table, eating Bonducci’s sandwiches and crushing a couple of Peroni’s. The quiet is driving Julia mad. The tension in the room is crushing her. She’s never seen Vinny so serious for so long. And she certainly has never physically been around while he is working. Of course, he wasn’t working. It’s just the three of them hanging out, just like they sometimes do; however, something is different this time. She's not sure what, but she can feel it. It's not a good feeling.

They all finish their sandwiches and clean off the table. "Where is Maria?" Sal asked after about twenty minutes of silence.

"I told her to take the night off. She's been working hard lately. Too hard. So I gave her a break. Besides, we need to talk business tonight, and I know that our business makes her… uncomfortable."

Hearing this makes Julia cringe.

"Oh yeah? What do we need to talk about tonight?" Sal asked.

"Business. We'll discuss it when the time is right," Vinny said without looking at Sal.

When they finish cleaning up, Sal and Julia sit back down at the kitchen table. Vinny grabs a bottle of his finest brandy and three glasses. He sits down, pours one for himself, one for Sal, and raises the bottle at Julia, looking at her questioningly. She shakes her head, so Vinny bypasses filling up the third glass.

8

Meanwhile, Joe and Tony have already arrived in Palermo, and are pulling into Vinny's driveway. Not in the Alfa Romeo, of course, but in Tony's Black Fiat 500. Joe hated the damn car, that's why they never took it anywhere. But Tony loved it. He thought it was practical. Good for the city, it being small and having good gas mileage. Their cars were probably the only thing in the world where Tony thought more practically than Joe.

Another car pulled up to Vinny's house behind the brothers but parked on the street. The boys didn't notice the car park behind them. They were too focused on the business they had to take care of tonight.

Just as Vinny was about to take his first sip of brandy, the doorbell rings.

"I'll get it!" exclaimed Julie, clearly excited to get out of the situation.

"Oh actually, babe. Could you fill up the decanter with water? We should stay hydrated tonight if we are to discuss business."

"Sure," she said gloomily. *Why is Vinny being so weird*, she wondered.

"Sal, I need to hit the Lou real fast. You mind gettin' the door?"

"Yeah. Sure," he replied.

Sal walks slowly through the foyer and to the front door. The beautiful, white marble door with golden knobs. Sal opens it and sees nothing but a small black hole. He's staring into the barrel of a handgun. Joe's handgun. Before he can say anything, he sees a flash of light, and then everything goes dark – black.

Vinny comes running to the front and looks at his white marble door. On the door, is pink brain matter, pieces of crushed skull, and dark red blood splatter painting it like a Jackson Pollock. He then looks down and sees Sal's limp body laying on the floor in his foyer with a red circle between his eyes. A shiny object on the ground catches his eye, and he bends down to pick it up. It's the bullet from Joe's gun. The chunk of metal is flat as a coin. The bullet went straight through Sal's skull and got crushed on the door.

Vinny holds the flattened bullet up in front of his face and says to his sons, "You see this? Not a hole in the door. Not a scratch. Just a flattened bullet." He then gestures towards the door. "White marble. A fine, strong rock. Much like Cosa Nostra, it will *never* break." Then he wraps his fist around the bullet and shakes it in front of his face. "*Nothing* from the outside can break our family."

They stand in silence for a few seconds, while Joe wipes blood from his smoking gun with his handkerchief. Then, Joe and Tony see their father's face turn pale.

They turn around to see what he is looking at and see Nicolette. She was driving the car that was parked on the street behind them.

"Nicolette–" her father began.

"Save it," she retorted, immediately. " I came to see it for myself. To see if you've actually changed like you claimed. Saying you've taken a step back in your role in the business, that you're loyal, that you *care*. I can see you clearly haven't taken a step down from the business. Is the other stuff true?"

"Well, yes I–"

"Doubtful," she answered for him. I don't see Julia around. Did you run her out of the house too with a different whore?"

"No, she's–"

"Probably," she answered for him again. " I came all the way from Paris to see it for myself, Dad. I'm glad as hell I did because now I know everything you said was *bullshit*."

Tony and Joe have their heads down, not wanting to get involved. They are close with their sister even though they are still involved with the family. It is *their* family, after all. But they also understood that Vinny is her *father*. She of course has different expectations – different standards – for her own father. Nonetheless, they didn't want the scolding Vinny was receiving, so they stayed quiet and kept their heads down.

"It's not bullshit, Nicolette I swear. Julia is right inside. *I* didn't kill Sal, it was Joe!"

"Whoa, whoa," said Joe. "I'm just a bystander here, no need to include me."

"*Bystander?*" Vinny retorted. "You pulled the goddamn trigger!"

Nicolette starts walking away, shaking her head and Vinny runs after her. He stands in front of her, grabs her shoulders gently, and says, "Nicolette, please believe me. I *have* changed, but what hasn't is the fact that I am still your father."

She looks him dead in the eyes and retorts, "No, you're not," and walks around him toward her car. Then without even looking back she yells, "You won't be coming to my wedding either, asshole!" giving him the bird.

Chapter 15

Cocoa, You Say?

It's a sunny April afternoon in Palermo, just one week since Sal passed (or more accurately, was murdered). Joe, Tony, and Sal are sitting poolside at Vinny's villa smoking cigars. Julia and Josephine are laying on inflatable tanning rafts in the middle of the pool soaking up the sun and sipping on Aperol Spritzes. The kids, Sara and Anna, are in the pool as well; however, they are not enjoying a nice relaxing tanning day. They are in a fight to the death, spraying each other with water guns, and laughing uncontrollably.

"Man, I haven't been this relaxed in over a year," said Tony.

"Yeah. When's the last time we all got together, and just enjoyed the day, eh?" said Joe.

"Well, your uptight ass sometimes makes it difficult sometimes, Joe."

Joe reaches under his pool chair, pulls out a water gun, and squirts Tony, once.

"Hey! Hey, I'm kiddin'. No need to be so trigger-happy," he said.

"Yeah, you're one to talk."

"Play nice, boys," said Vinny. "You're both a little trigger-happy. Nothing wrong with it."

They all three sit back and enjoy the summer sun blasting their dark, olive complexions.

There is nothing better than a day with the family.

1

Meanwhile, Giovanni Conti had been spiraling out of control. He lost his mother, brother, and father all within two years. It was too much to handle. Gio and Sofia both decided to let their apartment leases expire and stay with each other at the once-full Conti house. She couldn't leave Gio alone.

Much like his father, Gio became crippled by the dark grasp of alcohol. Unlike his father, he didn't try to hide it. It was clear as day for Sofia to see. He'd wake up still drunk, drink with his breakfast, drink with his dinner, and have a nightcap before bed.

She knew he couldn't continue like this, so she invited him to live with her parents at their home on the outskirts of Palermo. *He just needs community,* she thought. She was mostly correct. Having a community helped Gio a great deal. Her parents were incredibly welcoming, especially considering he had never met them. They drove him to his AA classes, made sure he was getting out of the house to meet with friends, and even made him enroll at a local University, which they paid for.

Over the years, he would fall off the wagon, and go on a binger at least once every two months for four years straight. It wasn't until he started his full-time career, that he found purpose again. Purpose, he came to find, is what provided him the ease to turn down a drink. Plus, his new job as an operative for the United States Drug Enforcement Agency European office, would require him to stay on the straight and narrow. The job kept him busy, so he didn't have time for a drink anyhow. But that's a story for another time.

Sofia finally published her debut novel titled *Sunsets*, which was a fiction novel inspired by her and Nick's love story. This wasn't her favorite project, but it was the only one she had that she felt was ready to publish. Her favorite one was the book she began in Vietnam. It was a fiction novel inspired by the stories Nick and Gio told her during her visit to the farm. Of course, she used fake names and dramatized a few parts, but it was fairly spot on to the events that transpired at The Palermo Coffee Company. Even though it was her favorite project, she didn't publish it. *Couldn't* publish it. She promised Nick to keep it to herself so his reputation with the family wouldn't get tarnished. He decided not to mention the part about it putting their lives at risk. At first, she was pretty upset with him. "Caring about your reputation so much is preventing you and everyone around you from reaching their full potential!" she'd say. Even though she was upset, she made the promise. He was the only person in the world that knew a detailed book about the family's operation existed. And that information died with him.

One year after Nick's death, Sophia began toying with the idea of publishing the book anyway. Yes, she made a promise to her sweet Nick, but a lot has changed since then. She wondered if publishing the book would give her the closure she so desperately needed. But that too, is a story for another time.

Back in the present time at Vinny's villa, the sun blared on. Joe asked, "So? What now?"

"Whaddya mean, 'what now?' You bored? Not enjoyin' yourself?" asked Tony.

"No, I mean. What now? As in what's our next operation?"

"I think we take some time off. An old man can use a break," said Vinny.

"You didn't even do anything, old man. What could you possibly be tired from?" asked Tony.

"Managing you assholes is exhausting," Vinny said, making all three of them erupt in laughter.

Once they settle down Joe says, "But seriously. If you're too tired, you know me and Tony can run the family, right, Pops?"

"I know, I know. You boys would do a fine job too. I just think we all need to be with our *actual* families for some time," he replied.

"Yeah, I guess you're right. But if anyone gets any good ideas, I'm all ears," said Joe.

Tony turns to Joe and says, “You know, I hear Cocoa farmers have been experiencin’ alotta price pressure lately.”

Hearing this, Joe turns to Tony and gives him a big, sadistic grin. He replies, “Cocoa, you say?”

THE END

www.ingramcontent.com/pod-product-compliance
Lightning Source LLC
LaVergne TN
LVHW010559100826
845148LV00014B/2767